A MAN OF IMPECCABLE Taste

R. BROOKE JEFFREY

iUniverse®

A MAN OF IMPECCABLE TASTE

iUniverse books may be ordered through booksellers or by contacting:

iUniverse
1663 Liberty Drive
Bloomington, IN 47403
www.iuniverse.com
844-349-9409

ISBN: 978-1-6632-0783-8 (sc)
ISBN: 978-1-6632-0784-5 (e)

Library of Congress Control Number: 2020924606

Print information available on the last page.

iUniverse rev. date: 01/20/2021

The past is not dead. In fact, it's not even past.

William Faulkner

To my three wonderful children: Catherine, Luke, and Elizabeth Jeffrey. A special thanks my sister, Lauralee Field and my sister-in-law, Andrea Stein, for their excellent editorial assistance.

Part 1

Paris, February 1, 1957

The novel has gained preeminence as a literary form in the West because it presents truths to us in the form of fiction that we cannot bear to confront in the reality of our lives. These truths inevitably reveal themselves when our fierce biological destiny clashes with pervasive societal constraints. It is therefore not surprising that the major theme of many of our greatest novels—*Ulysses, Madame Bovary, Anna Karenina*—involves the complex social phenomenon of adultery.

This topic was in the forefront of my mind when I was asked by the grieving widow of Freddy—my sergeant detective of sixteen years—to clean out his office file cabinets. In the course of our daily rounds, long lunches, and evening libations throughout central Paris, there was hardly a barmaid or shop mistress who was not immensely charmed by the curly-haired hulking bear of a man masquerading as a detective. It was therefore of considerable importance to me, as the custodian of his files, to meticulously expunge all letters, receipts, and mementos that could plausibly reflect reciprocated affections.

In the course of this marital reclamation project, I was forced to relive the many frustrations and occasional triumphs of the murder cases Freddy and I had worked on at the Central Paris Bureau. It was indeed quite a shock to find that, randomly dispersed throughout the files, there were also personal reflections at odds with the Freddy I thought I knew. They revealed him to be not only a poet of some lyrical sensibility but also a capable philosopher and lacerating observer of postwar politics.

My attempt to reconstruct the life of a man I thought I knew from these psychological fragments left me with an overarching sense of inadequacy. Beneath the facade of an outwardly comical and gruff alcoholic, Freddy was a man of subtle reflection and deep feelings. I suppose it follows that if we cannot come to understand our closest friends beyond mere superficialities, then it must be hopeless to try to come to terms with the mind of someone quite

1

different from us—in my case, a person with a homicidal mind. But that is the task before us.

It is true what they say about Paris in August; it is, in fact, a desert. And that is exactly why I find that month so extraordinarily appealing. Having spent time in Tunisia during the war, I know something firsthand about the desert. It is far more than an ocean of sand. Indeed, it is more a state of mind than a landscape. There is something terrifying and starkly purifying about a vast reality made up entirely of white dunes and azure sky. I have seen men go insane in a matter of days because of the desert's oppressive isolation.

A similar thing can be said of the unreality of empty Parisian streets and cafés in August. The unique "desert" character of the city at that time forces us to confront our true selves within the abandoned shell that creates the illusion of Paris. Within that abiding emptiness comes a radical simplification of one's life. Indeed, it can be more terrifying than a prison cell. Devoid of the quotidian meaninglessness of obligatory human interactions, the mind turns inward to encounter the striking void at the center of our being. Survival in such a harsh environment requires more than mere cleverness or cunning; it demands of us a psychic transformation akin to alchemy. Only a person with a passion for self-deception can survive the singular loneliness that is Paris in August.

The source of my own self-deception, and my one true passion, is food: classic French cuisine, to be precise. If civilization is to endure until the exhaustion of our solar system, it will not be the result of the engineering skills of our German friends or the self-congratulatory can-do attitude of our American colleagues. On the contrary, nature has ordained that it will be left to the French to preserve humanity—or, rather, to preserve what makes life worth living: art, music, and romance, to be sure, but first and foremost, nurturing and inspiring food. French cuisine, as with the great Homeric oral tradition, has been handed down with slight variations from generation to generation, while preserving at its core the essence of why roving bands of hominids instinctively chose to roast an antelope leg over a fire rather than eating it raw.

Putting aside this melodramatic digression, let me be blunt: in August, people with money leave Paris, and much like the symbiotic relationship between barnacles and whales, so do the criminals who cling to them. As a result, there is remarkably little work for me in my office as deputy chief inspector of police, homicide division. The August Parisian desert allows me the freedom to do my best work, which is painstakingly to catalogue and analyze my dining experiences from the previous winter at the Twelve Apostles, or the twelve greatest restaurants in Lyon.

One does not dine in Paris for the food. There is, in fact, no intrinsic Parisian cuisine. It is, in reality, merely an amalgamation of everything that misguided critics deem pretentious enough to be exported from the provinces. No, dining in Paris is almost entirely devoted to frivolity, showmanship, and feigned gaiety, all of which serve as an illusory antidote to the ennui of modern urban existence. If one wishes to explore the epitome of true French cuisine, one must consider Lyon and only Lyon.

The inescapable essence of *la cuisine Lyonnaise* is its simplicity. Take for example the humble *Solanum tuberosum*, or potato. When Marie Antoinette wore a headdress of purple potato flowers to a ball at Versailles, the French nobility suddenly realized what the Incas had known three thousand years before: namely, that the potato is the most regal of all vegetables. Prior to that epiphany, the potato in France was rumored to cause leprosy and was relegated to pigs' feed. It was left to the chefs of Lyon to create a place of honor for the potato in the cuisine of France. When one experiences potatoes cooked to perfection with the finest onions, butter, salt, and parsley fresh from the garden, it creates a degree of blissful release rarely approximated by other human activities.

To be certain, underlying this outward simplicity is a daunting complexity. It was Stendhal who said that in Lyon he had encountered twenty-two types of potatoes prepared in twenty-two different ways. Knowing precisely its peak of freshness and flavor for the exact potato of that day's meal is the foundational genius of *la cuisine Lyonnaise.*

I once read in a scientific journal how researchers at the North Pole had achieved great insight into both human history and the climate of the planet by observing chemical changes within rings of ice taken from small cores deep below the earth's surface. But why go to the North Pole when I can take the morning train to Lyon?

For the past twenty-five years (except during the war), I have taken my annual vacation every February in Lyon. Its rich hearty fare, I believe, is best consumed in the dead of winter, when there is little else to cheer one's soul. After dinner each night in my hotel, I assemble and catalogue my prodigious notes. Once back in my office in Paris, when I am afforded the perspective of time, I take the month of August to record all the slight variations of the culinary season in terms of classical technique, presentation, the balance of flavors, and the pairing of foods with wine.

This exacting process has afforded me a unique perspective on subtle, yet profound, trends in the evolution of French society. Much like mythology for Carl Jung, my hypothesis has always been that the classical culinary tradition of Lyon is foundational for the collective French consciousness. Indeed, I believe my longitudinal study reveals a unique insight into the transformation of our national psyche as valid as any rigorously performed scientific investigation.

It became evident to me that by the late 1930s, there was an emerging loss of confidence and indeed a growing malaise reflected in the gastronomy of Lyon. Gone was any attempt at real innovation or the execution of complicated dishes or pairings. There were lapses in technique. The boldness and brightness of its palette had diminished. There was a pervasive sense that the long-cherished traditional recipes were inadequate, yet there was no consensus of how to evolve and forge a new path forward.

How else can one explain the incomprehensible French military defeat in 1940, when two million of our soldiers surrendered to the Germans within a matter of weeks? Was this disgrace solely the result of the fact that France lacked a stirring wartime leader like Churchill? Or was it the case that we fundamentally lacked nourishment for our souls?

While my exploration into French cuisine may reveal the nature of our evolving society, it falls short as a study of individual human motivation. What ultimately rouses human beings to act? Why should one society create monumental art or build a pyramid while another builds a great wall? For that matter, why does another society build nothing more than a canoe? No doubt there are a myriad of factors—economic, genetic, and even aesthetic. But here is what I consider my great insight, or the equivalent of an "ice core" deep in the human psyche: the careful study of homicide—specifically, a study of its most violent and shockingly brutal cases.

During eleven months of the year, I have a comfortable set routine. Every morning at nine o'clock, armed only with a steaming cup of Moroccan mint tea, I enter my Paris office, hang up my jacket, and settle into my leather chair, brimming with anticipation. It is then that I am able to analyze—at my leisure—the glossy black-and-white forensic photographs that survey the previous evening's collective carnage of stabbings, shootings, hackings, and mutilations. As constant as the human need for food is the apparent need to annihilate our fellow human beings.

The cultural tradition of cuisine in Lyon is prized for its continuity and conservatism. Over long periods of time, the gastronomy of Lyon has been subtly influenced by slight variations in our evolving French societal character. The exact opposite is true of the extraordinary range of methods, means, and motives to commit murder. It might well be argued that homicide is, in fact, the wellspring of a never-ending source of human creativity. Even before beginning to understand the depths and cultural dimensions of this phenomenon, it is clear to anyone in the know that standard texts of criminology and psychology are of no use whatsoever. Apart from the aphorisms of Freddy, great characters from literature— from Macbeth to Raskolnikov—are by far the most useful key to understanding the complex motives of premeditated murder.

A fair question one might ask at this point is why someone from my background would choose to become a homicide detective. A man born into the slightly diminished, but nonetheless minor, nobility, and possessing superior academic credentials (no less a first-class law degree), is not the typical profile for this profession.

Unlike Freddy, I do not project an imposing physical presence. I am of average height, and my sinewy limbs do not hint at the fact that in my youth I was a tennis champion. My unruly red hair and round tortoiseshell glasses convey—even in my early fifties—a sense of youthful whimsy more than gravitas. I suppose this is why in unofficial communications within the office Freddy often referred to me as the "choirboy."

Speaking candidly, I do possess one psychological trait that I believe facilitates my career. At the insistence of my English mother, my early schooling was at an English boarding school. There I developed a certain sense of detachment and objectivity as a defense mechanism against the constant abuse I received as the "Frog" in their midst. This mindset may be felicitously applied to many professions, but it is essential when trying to unravel the intricacies of a brutal homicide.

The thought of my chosen profession was very much on my mind as I boarded the train in early February for my annual sojourn to Lyon. As I watched countless miles of gray countryside fade past Chartres Cathedral, accompanied by the repetitive staccato of the train tracks, it occurred to me that I was somehow drawn to the exacting finitude of the act of premeditated murder. My experiences in war, both in combat and in prison camps, had always involved a disorienting moral relativism. If, as an officer, I made one choice, then a certain number of men would die; if I made another, there would be a different butcher's bill.

The so-called "fog of war" is not just about the uncertainty of the ebb and flow of battle. It is more often our lack of clarity or insight into how, in the end, the fighting and the slaughter will affect our souls. Whatever else can be said about a corpse lying in a Parisian street with an ice pick through its carotid artery, for a detective, it is a sorbet for the psyche and an intensely clarifying act in an otherwise inherently random and chaotic universe.

◇————◆————◇

Murder is a grave business.
—A.L. (Freddy)

Homicide, by its nature, reveals a most basic and unambiguous form of human motivation. To be sure, the motivation for premeditated murder is a complex mosaic, but at its foundation lie several disturbing evolutionary questions. Why, as it has been since the time of Cain and Abel, do we so fervently wish for another human's demise? Why do so many of us dream of nothing else?

While there are classical patterns to homicide, variations and anomalies still abound. It is precisely in studying the exceptional case that we gather the greatest insight to unravel the complex threads that obscure our deepest desires and motivations. Such was true of the homicide case known as the "Crucifixion in Saint-Alban."

◇————◆————◇

It is inconceivable that the Nantua sauce for the poached *quenelles de brochet* would be served cold at Chez Manton in Lyon. That is why its headwaiter hesitated, waiting until the dish had been consumed and my palate had been cleansed with a second sip of the Mâcon-Uchizy, to discreetly pass the card on a silver plate informing me of a phone call from Paris.

I reluctantly rose from my table to respond through the phone, its cord outstretched, "Maillot here."

"Charles?"

"Yes, Chief?"

"You'll forgive the interruption."

"Sir?"

"We have an emergency. A crisis, in fact. Toulouse. Horrid business."

"Toulouse. Isn't that Albert's prefecture?"

"Yes, and we both know Albert to be a capable man, if he operates a bit by the book. But there's been a murder. Outside Toulouse. At the summer home of the archbishop. A gruesome business."

"I'm sure Albert can handle it, sir."

"Under normal circumstances, I would agree. But Albert has had to recuse himself. The archbishop has ties to Albert's father—significant financial ties that are best left undisturbed."

"I see. Well, recusal seems appropriate then, sir."

"The long and short of it is that Albert has requested that the Central Bureau take over to produce an initial report—a first go-round, but one that clearly exonerates the archbishop. Then, we can let Albert take over."

"I take it, sir, that you want me to interrupt my vacation, go to Toulouse, investigate the facts, and prepare a preliminary report in a week?"

"Exactly."

"Right. And why are we to exonerate the archbishop?"

"He's nearly seventy and confined to a wheelchair. I doubt he could do much damage to a plate of macarons, let alone crucify someone."

"Crucify?"

"Yes."

"As in the crucifixion of our Lord and Savior?"

"From what I understand, yes."

"My God, how horrible! Where again did this take place?"

"At the archbishop's summer residence, a village called Alban. It seems the victim on the cross was nailed to his door."

"I'm guessing that might be Saint-Alban, sir. Passable goat cheese, as I recall, but not much else to recommend it."

"That might be it. I suspect you'll want to go there first thing in the morning and clear things up for me. You'll need a car, so call the office for the authorization number."

"The archbishop, is he a friend of yours?"

"No, not especially. Not on a terribly personal basis. Just someone who needs to be above the fray. I wish to be clear on that: it's important that he be above suspicion. Can't let this ruin his distinguished career. And of course, given his connections in the ministry, we wouldn't want—"

"We wouldn't want an adversary for the open position at Justice, would we, sir?"

"You could say that. I'll expect your report in a week, and then you can get back to your sauces or whatever it is that keeps you in Lyon."

"Very good, sir."

Herodotus tells us that crucifixion was first employed by King Darius the First of Persia in 519 BC, when he nailed three thousand political opponents in Babylon to vertical stakes. Generally used for crimes of treason throughout the ancient Mediterranean world, crucifixion was not outlawed until AD 341, when Constantine decreed it too heinous for civilized people. The crucifixion of Christ by the Romans was typical of their use of this particularly barbaric mode of public execution to deter political dissent within the empire.

But what was the reason for the shocking crucifixion in Saint-Alban? What sort of a man could commit such a hideous crime? How on earth could an archbishop be even remotely involved? How could I manage to eat cassoulet? These and many other disturbing thoughts preoccupied me as I prepared to leave for the Languedoc.

◇

Local folklore has enshrined cassoulet as the iconic dish of the Languedoc. In 1355, the city of Castelnaudary was under siege by Edward, the Black Prince, during the Hundred Years' War. Starving townspeople gathered all remaining scraps of meat, including goose gizzards, pork rinds, and sausages, and poured them into a steaming cauldron of fava beans. As the apocryphal story goes, the hearty dish invigorated the defenders and enabled them to lift the siege. I personally subscribe to the theory that the Black Prince withdrew because he had a rather sophisticated sense of smell.

◇

I suspect at this juncture that it might be of value to state that my personal life, to the extent that it is relevant, is not a desert per se. For several years both before and after I returned from the war, I had been involved in a deeply committed and satisfying platonic relationship with Alessandra. Sandy, as I've always called her, was the widow of my best friend in law school, Allain. Her father was a left-leaning politician in Turin who had escaped Mussolini and the Fascists for Paris in the early twenties. Allain had been my doubles partner in tennis; we played together every Sunday at my club.

In 1930 at the height of the Depression, Allain committed suicide. I must admit that, despite all my years as a police detective, I can provide no useful insight into that form of self-destruction. It became clear, however, that Allain's brother had run the family business into the ground and had incurred a mountain of debt. For the next several years, Sandy struggled to pay off the loans.

Although I offered to repay them on numerous occasions, she always had refused.

After Hitler annexed Austria in 1938, I joined the army. Sandy and I had become extremely close. Had the world been normal, I have no doubt we would have married. But the world was far from normal. It was impossible to make a rational decision in the face of an irrational universe.

> Charlie, there are only two kinds of conversations men have with women. The first is when you tell them the godawful truth and then you suffer the consequences. The second is when you lie, and they know it, but you don't hurt their feelings. There's never been a man born who regretted the latter.
> —A.L.

I knew that if I had forced the issue, Sandy would have married me. However, I also knew how profoundly fragile her state of mind was after losing Allain. I lied and told her that I wasn't ready for marriage and that it would just have to wait for a year or so until the war was over. What I think I understood viscerally, if not intellectually, was that while it might be possible for her to survive the loss of one husband, the loss of two would have been an unbearable cruelty.

I was determined to avoid a melodramatic scene between us at the train station when I left with my division. On prior occasions I had always relied on my English mother's sensibility—that "stiff upper lip" nonsense. But real life is not a movie where one can rehearse one's lines and do it over again if the emotions are not what the director wants. I don't remember saying anything useful or comforting. It was all I could do to keep from crying.

Sandy's financial situation continued to deteriorate. A year later, while I was stuck at the Maginot Line, she and her small son were evicted from her apartment. She wrote to me and told me that while she loved me, she had to do what was necessary to survive. The next time I heard anything at all about her was many months later, from a mutual friend who told me she had gone to Geneva and married a wealthy Swiss businessman right before the war.

After the German invasion of France in 1940 and the collapse of our defenses, I fled to London with the Free French under de Gaulle. It was my strong suspicion, however, knowing the Parisian army officer corps as I did, that de Gaulle's Free French simply meant "Free-from-Fighting French." As I had dual citizenship through my mother, I enlisted in the British army, and in 1941 I found myself in North Africa, attached to the Ninth Australian Infantry Division defending Tobruk.

Amazing chaps, those Aussies. They could fight all day and all night with only a tin of potted meat and a can of warm beer. We were surrounded and cut off with little ammunition, but we held out against Rommel for two hundred forty days before surrendering. I was a prisoner in Tunisia for five months, before being shipped to camps in Italy and Germany. Perhaps because I was an officer who spoke fluent German (how else to read Freud and Nietzsche, or Heidegger, for that matter?), I was afforded mail once a month from the British Red Cross. There was little of my family left at that stage, just a few spinster aunts in Paris and Rouen. But it was that monthly packet of letters from Sandy that kept me alive through every conceivable physical and psychological trial the Nazis could inflict.

After the war, Sandy and I reunited in a platonic way. She and her husband had relocated to Paris, and every Sunday afternoon for several years Sandy and I would walk her dogs together in the Bois de Boulogne. We had only one rule: never complain about any event, person, or circumstance in our prior lives. We had established this rule very early after the war based on a shared understanding that we had experienced too many personal tragedies. Dwelling on those topics would lead to inconsolable sadness. Allain's death, my deprivation as a German prisoner, and her unfortunate marriage were just a few of the many topics that fell into that category. But we were still alive, and we loved each other in a way that seemed emotionally satisfying. Many of our close friends had died or were psychologically wounded from the war. From that vantage point, we had nothing to complain about.

We frequently discussed my latest murder cases. Sandy had a doctoral degree in clinical psychology, which thus afforded me two incalculable advantages in my work as a homicide detective. First, she understood what motivated women; second, she understood what motivated men.

◇

When Sandy died of ovarian cancer in 1950, a deep sadness pervaded my life. I simply could not function in my work, so I decided to take the one and only nonculinary vacation in my career. For no particular reason, I went to Monaco, where I found myself gambling for two weeks. Despite my best efforts, I won a small fortune. Concentrating on the cards right in front of me was all I could manage. Somehow, I suppose, it helped. When I returned to Paris, I walked the cobblestone streets of Belleville at night, giving all the money away to the hollowed-out reproductions of men sleeping silently under the bridges.

◇

To be frank, although I was initially distraught at the thought of abandoning my culinary hajj to Lyon for a murder investigation, there was one major consolation: I would be able to visit my old friend Oscar in Toulouse.

Though outwardly Oscar Dubois and I shared little in common, we had, it seemed, been thrown together on the great wheel of fate, a wheel that had stopped to deposit us for nearly eleven months in a German prison camp.

Oscar and I had known each other reasonably well as undergraduates at the Sorbonne. Oscar was a brilliant mathematician, but truth be told, he was more interested in cafés than in calculus.

During our student days, whenever one of us found himself seriously in debt (bar bills for Oscar's part, and restaurant tabs for me), we would occasionally team up to play high-stakes duplicate bridge in the salons of wealthy aristocrats or similar poseurs. I always found it to be an immensely satisfying method of fleecing the idle rich while enjoying a passable meal in the process.

During our time in Paris, Oscar, being a somewhat portly though diminutive figure, seemed older than his age with his beard and spectacles. Moreover, he gave one the impression of being a slightly disheveled bohemian in both his dress and manner.

Our approach at cards was always the same. We would appear to be distracted by our host's elegant surroundings and pay little attention at the outset. Invariably, we lost the first few games; then we doubled our bets and proceeded to clean house. This gambit worked only on individuals who did not know us and, therefore, served as only an intermittent reprise amid our chronic financial challenges.

Oscar's true passion—other than wrestling with Fermat's theorem—was chess, not bridge. He never played for money; he played only for the satisfaction of beating ranked European masters. Before the war, I saw him play only once. It was at a Christmas party at some professor's home. After having had far too much to drink, Oscar was summoned to the drawing room to uphold the honor of France in a chess match with a visiting Oxford grandee who was billed as a formidable European champion. Even in his debilitated state, Oscar dispatched the interloper with astonishing speed and with such nonchalance that the man departed proportionately shocked and humiliated.

In the late thirties, when war seemed inevitable, Oscar was among the first of our circle of friends to enlist. Within a short time, his superior mind became apparent, and he was appointed an officer. The French Army, I am afraid, typically ignoring Oscar's remarkable élan and fighting spirit, shunted him off into the meteorology corps. I later learned that Oscar was captured while retrieving a weather balloon miles behind enemy lines.

After my own capture in Tunisia, I was transported seemingly at random to small prison camps in Italy, but here there was never a shortage of rations, and I was never forced to do arduous labor. In January 1944, when it was clear the Germans were losing the Italian campaign, I was sent by train from Milan to Bavaria to spend the rest of the war in the massive prison camp at Moosburg.

I was overjoyed to encounter Oscar in the barracks shortly after I arrived. We hugged for many minutes, but my elation was tempered by my shock at the alarming state of Oscar's health. His dulled eyes were sunken into sallow cheeks, and his thicket of black hair was now thinned and gray. Given that he was stooped like a pensioner twice his age, I could see he had been suffering the effects of malnutrition for many months.

Because Oscar and I were officers, we were billeted in a different hut from enlisted men, but the rations were just as meager. The Germans did not require officers to work as laborers in the massive munitions factory at Moosburg, but Oscar and I found this morally reprehensible. We both volunteered for the night shift so that we could converse more freely while our guards slept. The nighttime had the added advantage of being bombed by the inept British, as opposed to the more precise daylight raids by the Americans.

Compared to my experience in Italian prison camps, the conditions at Moosburg were appalling. There were only two meals of thin soup per day with scarcely any protein. When I questioned him, Oscar revealed in despair that an increasing number of men had already died of starvation and disease.

The commandant of the camp, General Joachim Buchler, was a sadistic Nazi who could have been typecast as Himmler's double in a B movie by Leni Riefenstahl. Buchler possessed a high, tinny voice, unimpressively projected behind his massive spectacles. His effeminate persona clashed absurdly with his oversized riding boots. I came to learn at his trial after the war that he unsuccessfully had sold encyclopedias door-to-door in rural Bavaria during the Weimar days. One can only imagine the rude dismissals he must have received from legions of portly farmers' wives.

Oscar and I knew that by the winter of 1944, the Russian front was collapsing for the Nazis. In quiet conversation late at night, we nonetheless both feared that many soldiers in the camp might not survive the months before liberation.

On Wednesdays after the morning parade, the entire camp of four thousand prisoners would stand at attention while Buchler—with Wagner blaring on a phonograph—played chess against an imbecilic second lieutenant. Within a few minutes, the defeated lieutenant would leap from his chair, give the Nazi salute, and proclaim yet another total victory for the commandant and the Reich. The triumphant Buchler would then stroll among the front lines of assembled prisoners, gleefully pounding his riding crop as if to make a point of his racial and intellectual superiority.

Late at night in the barracks, Oscar and I discussed our limited options for escape and concluded that even if some of us did manage to get past the guards, most of the men were too weak to survive in the woods for even a few days. Oscar became worked into a state and began muttering over and over that we must do something. I had no idea what he was planning.

The next Wednesday during Buchler's perfunctory victory stroll, Oscar thrust through the front lines and shouted in perfect German, "I can defeat the commandant in chess!" In that dramatic moment, Oscar's act of defiance literally froze time for all the assembled men. It was as if we were witnessing a move on a massive surrealistic chessboard with a pawn thrust forward, attempting to checkmate the king.

Guards rushed to restrain Oscar, but he began shouting again until Buchler violently raised his riding crop and demanded, "What is the meaning of this arrogance?"

Once again Oscar shouted, "I can defeat the commandant in chess, and if I win, you must increase our rations in the camp!"

There was silence as the startled Buchler looked nervously at the ground. Then he spoke: "And if you lose?"

"I will not lose. But if I do, you can do with me as you wish!"

"Then we will settle this matter immediately!" shot back Buchler.

Two guards seized Oscar and roughly hustled him up the steps to the German officers' mess. We stood at parade for no more than fifteen minutes, a millennium to every man assembled. Suddenly Oscar emerged briskly, walking down the steps alone. His jaunty gait and upright posture announced to the world the outcome we had prayed for.

At that very instant, out of the gray skies came the low rumble of American bombers. Neither the crashing of bombs on the factory district, nor the guards' whistles, nor the alarm sirens could drown out the shouts of joy from four thousand men.

The results of the famous chess match were never revealed. Oscar never mentioned it either during or after the war. He didn't have to. The results were self-evident as rations were immediately increased. In the last few weeks, before the Russians arrived, Buchler was hardly visible in camp. That spring, Oscar and I were liberated together. We made the two-month trip back to Paris on foot, by farmer's cart, and by broken-down truck in squalid splendor.

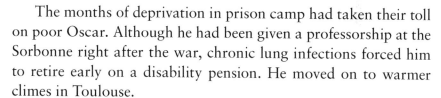

The months of deprivation in prison camp had taken their toll on poor Oscar. Although he had been given a professorship at the Sorbonne right after the war, chronic lung infections forced him to retire early on a disability pension. He moved on to warmer climes in Toulouse.

On several occasions after the war, I had met Oscar's sister Emma when they visited Paris together. A birdlike woman with severe features and tightly pulled-back hair, she was a classic bluestocking academic who taught classes in medieval history at Toulouse. The two lived together in a small farmhouse on the outskirts of the city.

I telephoned Oscar the morning I was to depart from Lyon and arranged to have dinner with him that night. Oscar insisted not only that I have dinner that night but also that I stay with them during my visit. I readily agreed to both propositions.

Throughout my journey, my thoughts alternated between the joy of being reunited with my old friend and the dread of having to deal with the inevitable bureaucratic entanglements related to murder at an archbishop's residence—and a grisly murder at that. Despite the extraordinary creativity and barbarism of Parisian thugs carrying out acts of murder, they had never delved into the complex realm of crucifixion.

Unlike many individuals, I quite enjoy driving long distances on country roads. The monotony of the countryside has always induced in me a rather languorous stupor, a most pleasurable anesthetic that transports me to my personal land of the lotus-eaters. I often find myself quite surprised to have actually reached my destination. In this semihypnotic state, my mind wanders in the most unpredictable ways, but it generally is guided along my two mental axes of food and death.

Between German artillery barrages in Tobruk, I distinctly remember a British archeologist going on about the ancient Egyptian custom of leaving bread and beer in the tombs of their deceased pharaohs and how they painted the walls with herds of fattened cattle and fantastic birds for the deceased to eat over the course of their journeys through eternity. Just last week in the paper was an article about the excavation of King Midas's tomb in Anatolia that referred in detail to the ornate dinnerware and silver chalices from a funeral meal that were sealed in his tomb.

Yet, as I pondered the details of the case I had been asked to solve, it struck me that the strangest confluence of food with death may be the Christian habit of Communion. Could not the partaking of the bread and the wine as early representatives respectively for the body and blood of Christ be construed as a symbolic way of always reminding the faithful of this gruesome death? Moreover, without the crucifixion of Christ and his subsequent resurrection, there is no doctrinal basis for Christianity. Over the millennia we seem to have forgotten the ideological centrality of the barbaric act of crucifixion to religion in the West. I suspect, however, for the perpetrator of the crucifixion in Saint-Alban, that the shock value of this crime in that location was foremost in his mind.

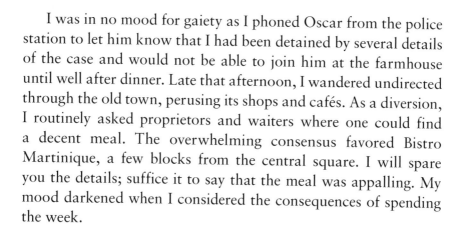

Once inside the city limits of Toulouse, I drove straight to the prefecture of police, arriving by late afternoon. I was greeted by Sergeant Guyton, who informed me that Albert, who was at the local hospital awaiting the birth of his first grandchild, had sent his regrets. We would instead have dinner the following evening at Albert's home. That suited me quite well, as now I would be free to have dinner that evening with Oscar and his sister. I arranged with Guyton to meet the following morning to review the state of play once I had had an opportunity to review the files.

Despite my many years of experience with grisly crime scenes, the photographs taken at Saint-Alban filled me with dread. There were nearly twenty pictures taken at different angles, some magnified, others shot from a distance. What they depicted was an elderly naked man with his hands and feet nailed to a large wooden cross that was positioned upside down against an arched doorway. While that in itself was shocking, the truly frightening aspect of the scene was a medieval-looking hand ax planted in the forehead of the victim.

I was in no mood for gaiety as I phoned Oscar from the police station to let him know that I had been detained by several details of the case and would not be able to join him at the farmhouse until well after dinner. Late that afternoon, I wandered undirected through the old town, perusing its shops and cafés. As a diversion, I routinely asked proprietors and waiters where one could find a decent meal. The overwhelming consensus favored Bistro Martinique, a few blocks from the central square. I will spare you the details; suffice it to say that the meal was appalling. My mood darkened when I considered the consequences of spending the week.

Much later that evening, after many missed turns on country roads and several misguided directions by misinformed but well-meaning farmers, I arrived at Oscar's farmhouse. As Oscar and his sister Emma were asleep, I was greeted by their housekeeper, a pleasant grandmotherly type who talked incessantly as she showed me to my room in an adjoining cottage and kindly brought me a baguette, some very agreeable local cheese, and a half bottle of quite acceptable red wine.

At breakfast the following morning in the farmhouse kitchen, Oscar and I embraced for a long, wonderfully heartfelt moment. The joyfulness of our reunion was tempered, however, by my shock at how rapidly Oscar had aged since the war. He was gaunt with thinning white hair, and deep labyrinthine crevices framed his sunken cheeks. His eyebrows had receded, and he spoke in a raspy whisper, punctuated by gasps for air. Our conversations strayed into tangential topics of the day as I hoped I could uncover from beneath his diminished exterior the clarity and wit of the old Oscar.

We briefly discussed the purpose of my trip, to investigate the murder at Saint-Alban, but we chose not to dwell too much on the gruesome details. It was an unusually fine morning in late February, so Oscar and I took our coffee out into the sunshine to sit at the wooden table beneath the pergola. It was so freakishly warm that, had the wisteria been in bloom, it was easy to imagine that we had been transported to the middle of May.

"Charles, do you recall another day like this in the dead of February when the sun was shining, and spring seemed somehow to burst upon us in winter?"

"No, not really. Weather like this never happens in Paris."

"But you must remember. It was a day just like this—a beautifully warm, sunny day in the dead of winter. It was the day the camp was liberated by the Russians."

"Oscar, I do believe you're right. What a memory! The snow had just melted. I remember standing with my ankles in mud on the parade ground that morning."

"It's funny what fragments of the past one retains. What I recall most vividly is the scene outside the German infirmary."

"The gauntlet. All the men screaming."

"Yes, exactly. Even when the Russians pulled up in their trucks with soup and all sorts of food, there was a group of prisoners who ignored the food and waited as the Russians brought out the few remaining Germans who were too sick to escape."

"I remember that scene with the Germans being dragged out between the two lines. Although the men were too weak to hit the Germans, all the men shouted in unison, 'Shame! Shame!'"

"Yes. I wonder what that tells you."

"Well, Oscar, based on my professional opinion, it tells us that, apart from sex, one clear abiding source of human motivation is the need for revenge."

"I suppose you're right. But what does an ax stuck in the forehead of a crucified man tell you?"

At that point, a high-pitched feminine voice filled the air from behind the kitchen screen door: "That Toulouse remains delightfully medieval!"

That outburst heralded the arrival of Oscar's sister Emma. Sitting down with her coffee, she exclaimed, "At some point, Charles, you might well benefit from hearing a historian's perspective on the rather tortured history of the Languedoc where the Catholic Church is concerned."

⬥

Without medieval Toulouse and, specifically, the Duke of Aquitaine, Odo the Great, one might be dining on beef tagine in Lyon rather than tripe cooked with onions. At the siege of Toulouse in 721, the attacking force of Saracens from Moorish Spain nearly succeeded in starving out the inhabitants of Toulouse. Lucky for us, Odo circled around the invaders at night and led a daring moonlit cavalry charge. The good duke routed the Arabs and saved the Languedoc for Christendom, sparing Lyon and yours truly from the ravages of turmeric and cumin.

⬥

Despite my most amicable efforts, the meeting with Sergeant Guyton after breakfast with Oscar was disturbingly inadequate on many accounts. Curiously, he presented the most shockingly gruesome murder to me in such a nonchalant manner that one would have thought it more a bicycle theft than a crucifixion with a powerful archbishop involved. Perhaps a certain amount of friction is inevitable when a so-called expert from Paris shows up to review one's case. Things started out poorly and went downhill from there.

"I noticed, Sergeant, that there isn't as yet a formal autopsy report?"

"Well, not as yet. The coroner is indisposed at the moment."

"Indisposed?"

"Yes, he is recovering in hospital, sir. Something about diverticulitis, I believe."

"And is there no assistant to perform an autopsy?"

"Not at the moment. Excuse me, Inspector, but with the ax splitting the man's skull, do you have concerns about the cause of death?"

"Well, perhaps not cause in this case—more in terms of determining the time of death and if there were any other internal injuries."

"Apart from the nails in the hands and feet, that is?"

"Yes. What can you tell me about the victim, Jacques Bisset, beyond what's in the file?"

"Not much, I'm afraid. Sixty-eight. Retired. Former caretaker and gardener at the children's hospital."

"In Saint-Alban?"

"Yes. He tended the garden there for many years until he retired. Still lived on a cottage on the grounds. Mostly kept to himself, I am told."

I got up out of the chair to stretch my legs, asking "No prior record? No obvious enemies?"

"None."

I began to sense a growing frustration in the officer and a

diminishing return on my questions, but I pressed on. "What about a wife? Any family?"

"None that we know of."

"A religious man?"

"Don't know, sir."

"Motive? Why would anyone want to kill such a man, let alone crucify him?"

"Not clear, sir."

"I see. As Winston once said, I believe we're dealing with a riddle wrapped in a mystery."

"Sir?"

"Any relevance to the cross being deposited at the door of the archbishop's summer home?"

"None that we have yet ascertained. The archbishop, as you might know, is retired and in poor health. Some sort of nerve damage to his legs. He's virtually an invalid."

"Right. And I see from the report that you've interviewed several local farmers, the archbishop's housekeeper, and staff at the children's hospital. Any leads so far?"

"No solid leads, sir."

"Anything you wish to add? Anyone whom you feel it might be of use for me to talk to at this point?"

"None that come to mind, sir."

"When may I see the body, Sergeant?"

"If you like, I can have Officer Weygand take you to the morgue. He was the officer called to the crime scene. What time would be convenient?"

"Now would be quite convenient."

"One final thing, sir. The chief inspector sends his regrets about dinner tonight. His daughter is still in labor."

My impression of the body was that it had belonged to a reasonably fit elderly man—a laborer by the look of his hands and ruddy face. Apart from an asymmetric leg length and a peculiar angle to his foot, there seemed nothing at first that was distinguishing. But as I lifted the sheet, I noticed that his genitalia were mutilated, and his testicles were missing.

"Officer Weygand, what do you make of the stigmata?"

"The what, sir?"

"The holes in the hands and feet."

"They're holes, sir."

"Yes, but do you see the difference between the holes in the hands and the feet?"

"Not really, sir."

"The holes in the distal tibias have drill marks, to make it easier to place the nails. The stigmata in the hands do not. Less bone to traverse. May I please see the nails?"

He showed me the nails on a display board. There were two different types.

"These upper nails were used to impale the hands, sir, and down below are the ones for the feet."

"Notice that the nails used to impale the hands are common carpentry nails with broad heads. The ones used for the feet are finishing nails. Notice the absence of the broad head. These are used for the construction of fine woodwork and furniture."

"Duly noted, sir."

"May I see the cross? The photos of it are somewhat obscured by the body."

"Of course. We will need to walk through this way to get to forensics."

"May I confirm that the photos listed as one through seven in the file were just as you found the undisturbed crime scene? It seems to me that the cross has been repositioned."

"No, sir. Those photos were taken by me at the crime scene exactly as I found it."

"Really? Because those pictures appear to depict the victim being crucified upside down."

"That is correct, sir."

I spent a fair amount of time examining the cross. It was exceptionally well-made of fine wood in a style that I did not recognize. Not the usual Christian cross with which I was familiar. Celtic perhaps. I asked the officer to take additional photos of the cross and have them sent to me that afternoon. I then spent the remainder of the afternoon walking the streets of the old town, trying as best I could to get some purchase on this whole gruesome matter. I succeeded only in wondering what Freddy would make of it.

The Hundred Years' War was a public relations rounding error. The English and the French fought for control of western France for exactly one hundred sixteen years, from 1337 to 1453. When the English conquered a charming hill town fortress in the Languedoc, they named it after Alban, the first martyred Christian in Britain to be made a saint.

The fourth-century Roman army occupying northern Britain fervently tried to eradicate all Christian priests as enemies of the gods of the empire. Alban, a Roman patrician, sheltered a fleeing priest in his home. He was so impressed by the priest's goodness, devotion, and piety that he converted to Christianity. When Roman soldiers searching for the priest entered Alban's home, he took the robes from the priest, offered himself up for execution, and was promptly beheaded. Immediately afterward, the executioner's eyes suddenly extruded from his head. Thus, the sleepy Languedoc hill town of Saint-Alban contains within its name the echoes of the extreme violence and passionate faith embedded within early Christianity.

I have worked with one—and precisely one—instinctively brilliant detective in my career in homicide, and that was Detective Alphonse Lemieux, the aforementioned Freddy. He saved my physical life on more than one occasion and also saved my professional life on an almost daily basis. Freddy somehow knew when to shoot first and ask questions later, as well as when to be restrained and pry open the door to find a widow with three small children.

Freddy faced life with two thematic approaches, humor and

alcohol, the two rarely in isolation and nearly always in abundance. But there was something else that I came to appreciate over the years about Freddy. If you were worthy of his respect, Freddy always treated you with respect, whether you were a hardened criminal, a Moroccan street cleaner, a butcher at Les Halles, or a woman of the night. Perhaps the most accurate statement I could make to sum up the man was to say that one simply felt good in his presence.

It might shock you to learn, however, that Freddy ardently believed that some murders were better left unsolved. While this notion might contradict one's theoretical view of justice, it was Freddy's conviction that the abstract administration of justice could, in fact, be contrary to the public good. I encountered Freddy's notion of justice in my very first murder case, one that I have often referred to as the Chesterfield Caper.

Hassan Moustafa was an outwardly amicable middle-aged Algerian who ran a small tobacco shop on rue Vincennes, which was located midway between our precinct headquarters and our favorite lunchtime bistro, Café Victoire. Freddy had spent the entire war in a German prison camp and had grown up near the endless rows of white crosses in Normandy. As a result, he was a great admirer of the Americans, and he much preferred the US brand of cigarettes, Chesterfields, to the ubiquitous Gauloises.

Conveniently, Hassan's shop was one of the few in Paris that regularly carried that American brand at a reasonable price, so we routinely stopped there on our way to lunch. Hassan was a solicitous shopkeeper, always quick with a story and facile in the sort of way that privileges the day-to-day chitchat of the workingman's Paris. He was known, however, to have a rather pronounced dark side. When drunk, Hassan violently beat his wife and two girls. It was not uncommon for me on my frequent trips to the hospital morgue to notice his wife or daughters in the accident ward as I entered, their swollen and bruised faces shrouded by their muted scarves.

On the morning of an unusually chilly day in March, Hassan's body was found on the pavement beneath his fourth-floor apartment, covered in clotted blood and glass fragments from a large bay window. I was designated to investigate his death.

Within half an hour of receiving my new assignment, Freddy strolled by my desk with his overcoat in hand and announced, "Charlie, we have an important matter to attend to. Let's go clear up this Hassan business, shall we?"

Presently we were ensconced in the Moustafas' apartment above their shop. Freddy immediately took over: "My sincerest condolences, madame. Of course, mere words at this time are terribly inadequate to convey one's profound sense of grief at your loss."

Her heavy makeup and a scarf did not fully conceal the purplish contusions over her cheeks.

Hearing no response, Freddy continued. "I'm afraid that because of our line of work, madame, I must ask certain rather delicate questions. Respectfully, I will be brief. Please be assured, madame, that your responses will be treated with utmost sensitivity."

Madame Moustafa seemed completely bewildered by the entire scene.

"Are you aware, madame, of certain debts your late husband incurred at the hands of a number of unscrupulous business associates habituating rue Lafarge?"

"Debts? What is the meaning of this? What are these debts?"

"Are you also aware, madame, of certain bank loans, unpaid loans from the Bank of Orléans in 1949 and '51? They total almost two thousand francs."

"Loans? My husband never told me about any loans. I handled all the money from the shop, Chief Inspector. I don't think Hassan ever walked into a bank."

"Ah, there you see, madame, the shame involved in all of it. The shame, the constant worry, the profound misery of financial dependency. It's what happens when a good man finds he cannot provide for his family. It's that shame, you see, that feeds the depression, the despair."

"Despair?"

"And the suicidal thoughts that inevitably follow. Plain as day, wouldn't you say, Charles? A man makes a few well-intentioned mistakes. He tries to cover them up. He gets a bit more money on the side merely to help his family. Gifts for the children, vacations perhaps. Then it all comes due."

"Gifts? We never went on vacations. There were no gifts."

Undeterred, Freddy persisted, saying, "But it's all so recognizable, madame, in our line of work. The dishonor, the depression, the feeling that the only freedom and release from the sorrows in this world is to be obtained from leaping out the window. To leap into the abyss!"

"Sorrows? What is the meaning of this, Inspector?"

"The motive, madame. The motive is as clear as day. A suicide, plain and simple. We shall trouble you no more in this matter in this hour of your grief. But may I, before we leave, inquire discreetly if you plan to keep the tobacco shop open, madame?"

"Of course, Inspector. It is our only source of funds."

"And the Chesterfields?"

"I will continue to order them especially for you, Inspector, without fail, the first Monday of every month."

"Very well! The matter is closed. Even in this grave hour of profound anguish, how wonderful to observe a certain continuity, a certain stability, that provides humankind with a measure of harmony—dare I say, reassurance—in our little universe."

"Harmony. Yes, I suppose that would be good."

And that was the end of it. Hassan's death was recorded as a suicide. The world took little notice. The tobacco shop continued to supply Freddy with his Chesterfields, and Madame Moustafa's formerly terrified daughters returned home in complete safety.

For Freddy the concept of "justice" was not an immutable or abstract legal theorem. To him it represented a workable, if inherently imperfect, compromise that shaped the lives of real people. I can only liken it to what Freud claimed was the stated goal of psychotherapy: to convert hysterical misery to common unhappiness.

Before he drank himself to death at fifty-two, Freddy and I visited a favorite bistro in Montmartre for steak frites to celebrate our modest year-end bonuses.

"Charlie," he said, "my judgment may be failing me in my old age, but you're probably not quite as hopeless as I first thought. But you're too impatient. The reality is that for the difficult ones—the murder cases with no motives, no suspects, and no evidence beyond a dead body—you've got to let the case come to you. A well-placed tip is far more useful than any of your so-called 'deductive reasoning.' Don't discount any angle. Remember, this is not like dating a woman. First impressions don't count. Most impressions are wrong anyway. Only the final guilty confession counts. But you've got to work both an inside game and an outside game."

He died before he could fully explain that last statement to me. Over the years, I have taken it to mean that you must fight your internal instincts and prejudices until the painstakingly constructed mosaic of the evidence reveals the entire picture.

Until it doesn't.

I phoned Oscar later that afternoon to say that I would be working late at the Central Bureau, going over all the interviews and the reports, and could not join them until later. I was most eager, however, to obtain a restaurant recommendation in town to avoid my earlier disappointment.

"Knowing you as I do, Charlie, there is only one choice: l'Hôtel de la Paix, rue des Fontaines. About a ten-minute walk from the police station. Don't miss the poulet de Bresse."

The thought of that meal, I admit, did cause me to end my investigations a bit early. I kept looking at my watch until half past seven, at which time I closed the office and headed toward the hotel. I can assure you that I was most surprised and delighted on many accounts.

The roast chicken with haricots verts and au gratin potatoes was traditional fare, but this incarnation was remarkably sophisticated in its execution. As in the finest tradition of Lyon, it was cooked perfectly with superior ingredients, a heavenly crisp skin, a deliciously savory pan sauce, and masterful seasoning with thyme and sage.

I had concluded that as much as I would enjoy spending time with Oscar at his farmhouse, it would be far more efficient for me to be located in the center of Toulouse. I left the restaurant and inquired at the front desk if there were any available rooms. As it was still late February I was in luck. Immediately, I moved my base of operations to the hotel. Before falling asleep, I made a note to myself to arrange an interview with the archbishop the next afternoon at his country house, the aforementioned crime scene.

My meeting—or, rather, audience—with the archbishop was as mystifying as it was brief. His summer "residence," located at the edge of the hill town Saint-Alban, boasted an impressive wood-framed exterior reminiscent of a Tudor style. The interior was a lavish palace overflowing with sculptures and paintings. We took coffee into an oak-paneled study that could easily have doubled as a men's club in London. The grandeur of the place put me off my game. It seemed perhaps the archbishop was interrogating me, rather than the other way around. Dressed in a simple priest's frock, he sat upright in his wheelchair with a tartan blanket over his legs. His perfectly coiffed white hair and large spectacles projected the practiced demeanor of a patrician barrister.

"I am indeed sorry," he began, "that you have been dragged into this sordid affair, Inspector. I am quite certain my friend Albert could have sorted it all out, but apparently that wouldn't do. As you can see by my present state, my legs are rather useless to me. Peripheral neuropathy, they say. I can assure you that I know nothing of this affair beyond the fact that this criminal act involves my property."

"Yes, and let me be clear, Your Excellency, there's no consideration of your being a suspect."

"Tell me, Inspector, what kind of barbarian would do such a thing? I mean to a harmless old fossil like Jocko?"

"By Jocko, you mean the victim, Monsieur Bisset?"

"Yes. I have known him for years. The gardener at the hospital. A cripple since childhood. A bit of a recluse, but charming to everybody. The children at the hospital adored him. As did I, Inspector. Some people said we even looked alike, if you can imagine that. You'd always see him around on market days and such. A kind of village idiot, I suppose, although that sounds a bit unkind. Saint-Alban is quite a small place, you know."

"From your perspective, would there be any motive for someone to kill him or, for that matter, to execute him in such a terrible fashion? Was he involved in any conflicts with anyone in the village that you might be aware of?"

"Conflicts? Absolutely not."

"And the religious dimension to all this, the crucifixion. Could you possibly shed some light on that? Was there any religious strife in the village?"

"Certainly not, Inspector. This is a very devout community."

As the conversation lagged, I began to become more aware of the large number of paintings in the study, all of which seemed to be portraits of an odd assortment of characters. As far as I could tell, the main subject matter was children and dwarfs.

"Quite an impressive array of paintings you have here. Rather interesting subject matter. Are they all done by the same artist?"

"Thank you, Inspector. Mostly just reproductions, I'm afraid. A few old masters thrown in, but, yes, there are a number by the painter Velázquez. He's rather a passion of mine. I acquired these over a number of years during visits with my ecclesiastical friends in Seville. They are quite engrossing, are they not? Pity he was a Jew."

"Seems that many of the portraits depict people who are—"

"Not quite right? You see, that's because they are dwarfs, Inspector. They were the companions of all the children you see here. King Phillip the Fourth had over a hundred dwarfs in his palace court. Imagine that retinue. Velázquez was his court painter and was drawn to all sorts of anomalous children and deformed small creatures."

My day from that point progressed steadily downward. The lack of reports and photographs to review contributed to my distinct impression of a lack of urgency by the police in this matter. That evening at the hotel, however, I was treated to another thoroughly successful meal of duck à l'orange. Afterward, I found myself in the small library just off the reception area. Over a glass of cognac, I began to reflect that, despite the gruesome nature of my professional business in Toulouse, I was fortunate to be reunited with Oscar. Additionally, I counted myself quite fortunate to have the opportunity to dine in this little jewel of a hotel.

As I pondered these thoughts while sipping my cognac, a waiter silently appeared to inform me discreetly that the bar would be closing. He offered, "Would you care for anything further, sir?"

"No, thank you. It remains only for me to have you convey my sincere congratulations to the chef for such a splendid meal."

"As it happens, monsieur, the chef is just leaving and is waiting for a taxi in the lobby. Perhaps you would like to express your compliments in person."

"Yes, indeed."

I rose quickly and sauntered into the lobby. Turning to meet me at the front desk in a gray cashmere cardigan, a black-and-white-striped blouse, and a scarlet scarf knotted at the side of her neck was the most stunningly beautiful woman I had ever seen in my life.

As the hotel's chef turned to meet me, I began, "I wanted to just say how—"

"How surprised you are to learn that the hotel chef is a woman?"

"Oh, not at all. I've just come from Lyon, where all my favorite restaurants have women chefs."

"Really?"

"Yes, I am a devoted acolyte in the church of les grandes mères Lyonnaises. Allow me to introduce myself: Charles Maillot. Inspector Maillot, Paris. I just wanted to compliment you on the excellent standard of the cuisine at the hotel. I'm staying here this week, and ..."

She managed a restrained smile. "Well, in that case, thank you. I'm Françoise Arnaud."

"Might I offer you a drink in the library, Chef Arnaud?"

"That's very kind, Inspector, but I must be at the market very early tomorrow, and I believe my taxi is here."

"Of course. A very good evening to you."

It has been my observation that the concept of feminine beauty inevitably incorporates not only physiognomy but also the elusive quality of style. Cultural norms of beauty are therefore the result of highly specific amalgams of these two factors. To make this point, let us contrast the aesthetics of feminine beauty between the English and the French. The concept of a beautiful woman in London incorporates a rather silly notion of overwrought vitality that is entirely foreign in Paris. There are, furthermore, unapologetic references to class distinctions in London (e.g., ridiculous hats at horse races) that are deemed déclassé on the Continent.

The indispensable quality of French style can be epitomized in the scarlet scarf that Chef Arnaud wore. Her gray cardigan and black-and-white silk blouse were as beautifully paired as foie gras with Sauterne. However, the accent of the scarlet scarf created in my mind a third dimension that transcended the plane of mere loveliness and took one to a realm of timeless idealized beauty.

Returning to the library after my invigorating encounter, I could not help but reflect on the singular importance of women in advancing French cuisine. While the patriarchy that is Parisian gastronomy worships at the altar of Escoffier, without Catherine de Medici's marrying King Henry II in 1533, French cuisine might not have progressed beyond pot-au-feu. No, it was Catherine who elevated French cooking to an aesthetic realm beyond mere sustenance and firmly established it with its own distinctive *arte culinária.*

Catherine and her army of Italian chefs introduced to France crystal glassware, fine glazed dishes, napkins, flower arrangements, embroidered tablecloths, and the fork. She was the first to separate savory from sweet, to understand the importance of vegetables, and to create sauces for both meat and fish. But that was a mere trifle compared to the myriad of dishes she introduced, from onion soup to duck in orange sauce. The concept of a banquet (she once served sixty-six turkeys) merely to entertain soon became a courtly obsession. And, of course, where would we be without macarons?

Part 2

It is a fair question to ponder why Lyon emerged as the indispensable epicenter of French gastronomy. There are two overriding historical factors. The first is the silkworm.

In 1540, King François, in order to punish the rebellious city of Genoa, granted Lyon a royal monopoly on all silk imports from China, making Lyon the final destination for the Silk Road. Over the next three centuries, Lyon flourished as the preeminent European center of silk weaving. By 1870 there were over one hundred thousand Jacquard silk looms, working day and night, centered in the Croix-Rousse district of Lyon.

Masses of silk workers, or *canuts*, coming off their night shifts congregated in a new and informal type of restaurant unique to Lyon, *les bouchons*. These modest places served hearty fare with three-course meals and wine beginning at nine in the morning.

The second factor in the triumph of Lyonnais cuisine was the emergence of the great female chefs of the *bouchons*, the pioneering culinary mothers, *les mères Lyonnaises*. It was the genius of these women to transform, over time, simple workingman's fare—such as eels cooked in wine sauce—into the foundation of haute cuisine. None was more famous than the celebrated Mère Brazier, who garnered no fewer than six Michelin stars.

The police files held astonishingly little information about the victim or a possible motive for his murder, let alone a crucifixion. There were no witnesses and, frankly, nothing of substance to go on. The autopsy report had not been completed. It seemed at the moment that the most plausible explanation for why a crucified victim had been deposited at the archbishop's front door was that it was the work of alien creatures. It was time to retrace my steps.

The victim, Jocko, by all accounts, had been associated with the Saint-Alban Orthopedic Hospital for Children all his adult life. Therefore, the hospital was my first stop.

After taking the turnoff from the river, I drove upward along a winding road lined with cedars. In due course I came upon the grounds of the hospital and its commanding main hall. While

I am no expert in historical architecture, the hospital gave me the impression of a grand palace with its formal gardens, ornate fountains, and sweeping marble staircase. Dr. Remy, the man in charge, ushered me across the inlaid oak floors into his office. He was a distinguished, earnest-appearing man with gray hair and blue eyes. In his starched white coat, he seemed very official in his demeanor. I was eager to learn the history of this extraordinary place.

"This main building," Dr. Remy explained, "was built in the mid-nineteenth century by the Duke d'Antoigne, a wealthy Parisian aristocrat who loved the climate here and this little hillside looking over the river and the valley. He used it mostly as an escape from rainy Parisian winters. At one time, the estate was truly enormous. The duke owned all the property you see around us on this hill, as well as all the land surrounding the river for nearly five miles. So, quite an impressive holding."

"How did it become a children's hospital?"

"In the 1880s, the estate was sold to a wealthy English aristocrat, a Lord Worthington. It was his wife who had the idea of turning it into a children's hospital in the 1890s. It was quite unusual in its time—a privately chartered hospital that specialized in the treatment of neuromuscular and orthopedic disease. In its heyday before the First World War, there were nearly a hundred children here from all over France and a clinical staff of about fifty nurses and doctors. The endowment paid for most of the patients' expenses. So, it was an impressive operation. It had its own surgical operating rooms as well."

"And what became of it? What is it now?"

"It's primarily a rehabilitation facility at the moment. The war changed things quite a bit. It now operates on a much smaller scale. Most of the estate's landholdings along the river were sold off after Lady Worthington died, right before the war. Having said that, the hospital is still quite functional and stays true to its mission of caring for children with neuromuscular problems. But it is no longer privately owned. It's now run by the local government in the department of Haute-Garrone."

"I see. Tell me, were you acquainted with the victim of this crime, Monsieur Bisset?"

"Of course, everyone knew Jocko. I'm relatively new here though—going on only about five years—and he retired shortly after I arrived. Very pleasant sort. Kept to himself mostly, but he loved telling a story. Always bringing some sort of treat for the children. Still puttered around the grounds and helped with the vegetable garden until the end. He certainly was well-liked by everyone as far as I could tell. That's why this has been such a shock to the staff."

"And he still lived on the premises?"

"Yes, he lived in a small cottage next to the orchard. I can take you to it if you'd like."

"I'm afraid I have taken up much of your time. Perhaps there is someone on your staff who knew Jocko well and might accompany me to his cottage?"

"Of course. The Kunstels are a Dutch couple who have been working here since the early thirties. I believe they might be of some help. Mr. Kunstel is our head gardener. He oversees a small crew that takes care of the formal gardens, and he has a large carpentry and repair shop. He and his wife live here in an apartment in the main building. Ada oversees the kitchen. I'll see if they're about."

Ada Kunstel was a tall, rather plain, slender woman with close-cropped brown hair and a loquacious manner. We chatted as we walked down the hill toward the cottage.

"I understand you knew Jocko well?"

"Of course, he was a fixture here. Tended the orchard and vegetable gardens forever, it seems—right up until his sixties, when he could no longer do the manual part of trimming the trees. But he still kept tending the vegetable garden. Every afternoon Jocko would stop by with a basket of fruit or whatever was in season. Always bringing peaches or strawberries to the children. Then he'd have his glass of *vin ordinare* on the terrace."

"Not the sort of man to engender any hostility, I take it?"

"Absolutely not, Inspector."

"Was he working here when you arrived at the hospital?"

"Oh yes. I believe he was one of the very first workers Lady Worthington hired."

"Lady Worthington?"

"That's right. I believe Jocko was a patient here as a child. Afterward, as a teenager, he became a sort of apprentice gardener, and subsequently he became head gardener."

"Fascinating that he was a patient here."

"Oh yes, that's been quite a tradition, it seems. A number of former patients over the years have stayed on to work here, like Jocko. I suppose it was hard for them to get regular jobs. Lady Worthington sought to employ them, perhaps out of pity, but who knows. It created quite a bit of loyalty among the staff knowing she would take care of them."

"I see."

There was nothing particularly remarkable about the cottage: a simple stone hearth that seemed to serve as the kitchen and an attached bedroom with a small cot.

"The picture on the mantel. Is that of Lady Worthington?"

"Yes, that's correct. Along the main corridor you can see a number of historical photographs of her that document both the conversion of the estate into the hospital and the building of the gardens."

"So, then, it was Lady Worthington who built the impressive gardens?"

"Yes. She loved the children and the gardens equally, it seems. There's a little library off the main corridor that has all the original plans and documents of all the buildings and the creation of the gardens. There are many old paintings of Saint-Alban as well. We could go there on your way out."

"Perhaps another time. I'm sure it's fascinating. I did have one question about the gardens though. I admit no expertise here, but my mother is English, and it's not a style that I associate with an English garden."

"Quite right, Inspector. It's not English at all. Done in the Italianate style with all greenery and no flowering plants. Much like you'd see outside of Rome. They were designed by the famous Italian landscape architect Domenico de Silva."

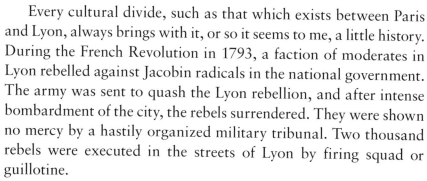

Every cultural divide, such as that which exists between Paris and Lyon, always brings with it, or so it seems to me, a little history. During the French Revolution in 1793, a faction of moderates in Lyon rebelled against Jacobin radicals in the national government. The army was sent to quash the Lyon rebellion, and after intense bombardment of the city, the rebels surrendered. They were shown no mercy by a hastily organized military tribunal. Two thousand rebels were executed in the streets of Lyon by firing squad or guillotine.

Shortly before he was executed, a priest was asked by the head of the tribunal whether he truly believed there was a hell. He replied, "No. Not until I met you."

Fortune may favor the brave, Charlie, but fortunately most of us aren't brave. No, it's the terrier who sinks his teeth into the postman's trousers who gets ahead in this godawful world.
—A.L.

I couldn't sleep that night. I kept seeing Françoise's blue eyes and her luxurious black hair with streaks of gray pulled back from a face that would have turned Botticelli's head. I needed to do something. The next morning at four thirty, I somehow found myself wandering around the stalls in the central market. I knew her first stop would be the fishmongers. My inspector's badge and more than a few well-placed francs had me sitting at her customary window table at Café des Halles, having ordered her usual almond croissant and café au lait.

She entered precisely at five o'clock. "Well, this is a surprise,

Inspector. I hope I'm not under suspicion for anything, other than perhaps a fallen soufflé."

"Not at all, madame. Please join me. I've taken the liberty of ordering breakfast for us."

"That's very thoughtful of you. To what do I owe this visit from a Paris detective at five in the morning?"

"Purely a social affair. I am devoted to Lyonnais cuisine and I sensed an immediate connection with your style of cooking."

Sipping her coffee, she responded, "Well, that's quite interesting. I worked in Mère Brazier's restaurant for nine years. But that still doesn't explain why you're here at this hour."

"An indulgence of mine. I wanted to observe a master chef at work, to see firsthand how she chooses the finest ingredients in the market. I am here only for a few days, and I promise you I will not be a bother. As silent as the grave."

Françoise leaned back, somewhat caught off guard, as the waiter brought her customary apricot jam.

"You are clearly a man who attends to details. Very well then. It shouldn't take up too much of your time, as in winter we have relatively few options. I hope you have passion for root vegetables, Inspector."

As we walked through the fishmongers' stalls, she spoke on a first-name basis to all the vendors. First came the shellfish and the sole, then the redfish, and finally the eels. All the while, she jotted down in her book what she had ordered to be delivered to the hotel.

"Aren't they beautiful? It's not just Brittany and Paris that get the finest seafood. These are all fresh from the rivers in the Dombes."

I leaned my head behind her shoulder. "Do you mind, madame, if I offer an observation?"

"Not at all, Inspector."

"The third eel that was chosen?"

"Yes?"

"The eyes were glassy. I'm afraid it is not fresh."

When my observation about the eel in question was confirmed, the entire tenor of our stroll was transformed. We held engaging yet polite discussions about the merits of root vegetables and the superiority of black truffles over white truffles.

Halfway through the market, we stopped to have coffee. I offered my favorite story about dining at Mère Brazier's restaurant.

"It was, of course, all related to her signature dish of chicken with truffles in pig's bladder, the famous poularde de Bresse en vessie. The chief inspector and I were dining with the minister of justice, a pompous man who was overly formal in his manner and speech. It started out to be a rather tense affair. The waiter, as it turns out, was a rough sort of character with a thick Provençal accent. When he cut into the pig's bladder, the chicken broth shot clear across the table and splattered the minister's tie. Without missing a beat, the waiter lifted his enormous eyebrows and, while wiping the minister's tie, said in an earthy baritone, 'Ah, but monsieur, this is a sign of extraordinary good fortune! It means you will certainly have your way with the ladies tonight.' After a tense few seconds, the minister roared with laughter. The rest of the meal was a smashing success."

Our stroll through the rest of the market was also a success. That evening, after yet another wonderful meal at the hotel, I waited for Françoise in the hotel lobby, this time with a glass of champagne in hand.

When I spied her, I sprang forward with two glasses. "Now may I offer you that drink?"

"My taxi seems late tonight. So, yes, thank you, Inspector."

And that became our little routine. Breakfast at five at the Café des Halles, a stroll through the market with intense food discussions, my dinner at the hotel, and a nightcap in the hotel lobby.

◇

My homicide case was progressing far less satisfactorily and seemed impenetrable. By the end of the week I was at an impasse. There was no motive for the killing, nothing in any of the interviews that hinted at any reason why someone would want to kill the old man. There were, of course, no witnesses. There were no fingerprints on the cross. It was hard to tie any of this to the archbishop. Albert, who was spending most of the time with his new grandson, was of little help.

That evening during my dinner drink with Françoise, a waiter entered the library to inform her that her taxi had been delayed by a flat tire and to ask if he should call another taxi company. Without hesitation, I offered Françoise a ride home. To my surprise, she accepted.

I stopped the car outside her small but charming stone house on the outskirts of the ancient hill town of Béziers. Françoise began the conversation.

"Charles, I've really enjoyed our time together these past few days.

"It's been such a pleasure to share my thoughts about food with someone who is equally passionate. But I want to be very clear: we're not children, Charles. It's important for you to know that our friendship will have to remain just that. I lost both my brother and my fiancé in the war. My sister and I spend what little free time we have taking care of my father. He's in his seventies and quite frail. The war has left an enormous hole in my heart. I hope you can understand."

"I do understand, Françoise. Like you, I've lost close friends in the war. And the only person I've ever loved was married to another man and then died of cancer. A friendship centered on our common interest in cuisine sounds very appropriate to me. I would welcome it."

It is a fool's errand to delude oneself into thinking that such a complex human emotion as the passion that inspires homicide can be understood or even analyzed from a logical perspective. Given my many years of devoted study, I confess a natural tendency to do so, despite all the inherent limitations, and to offer an intellectual framework, much as an artist makes a few preliminary sketches.

If we accept the first premise that premeditated murder is primarily a crime of passion, then the second premise we must confront is that the more gruesome the crime, the more passionate the motive. My third precept is that the more intense the motive, the fewer the likely suspects; hence, the easier it is to solve the crime. A fourth tendency is that to impose a rational framework on a fundamentally irrational act such as murder may indeed invalidate the first three axioms. In that case, an overarching logical framework for the crime must be abandoned.

A final and rather curious observation about premeditated murder is that most criminals desperately desire to be caught— not without a stirring chase, mind you, but caught just the same. They not only return over and over again to the scene of the crime, but they also express great relief once I handcuff them. You see, once a crime of passion has been committed and that crime has been widely publicized as being investigated by the police, the criminal can scarcely think of anything else (as Raskolnikov so aptly demonstrates). It becomes all-encompassing and takes over the perpetrator's entire psychic existence with a toxic alchemy of guilt, fear, anxiety, and anger.

<hr/>

The following week back in Paris I found myself lonely and dissatisfied. I had produced the required initial report stating that the archbishop was not a suspect, but apart from that, I'd offered nothing else. I was uneasy not only about the case but also about how I had left things with Françoise.

I was having a late lunch at my local bistro, when I was informed by my assistant Georges of an urgent call from Toulouse. I hurried back to the office.

"Is this Inspector Maillot?"

"Yes."

"This is Dr. Koblenz from Toulouse, chief coroner. First, I wish to apologize that my office was not able to complete the Bisset autopsy in a timely manner owing to my illness. Second, I am afraid that things are not what they seem."

"In what way, Doctor?"

"The cause of death was a coronary occlusion with a massive heart attack."

"The hatchet to the skull?"

"A superficial wound. It only partially penetrated the frontal bone and did not involve the brain itself."

"And the crucifixion?"

"There was no apparent hemorrhage caused by the nails in the adjacent tissues. It appears that this man died of a heart attack. The wounds from the hatchet and the crucifixion occurred at some point later in time—perhaps six to ten hours afterward."

———◇———

It's not whether we will face the abyss, Charlie. Whether we will do an about-face is all that matters.
—A.L.

It was time to take the chief out to his favorite restaurant for lunch and present my thoughts frankly.

"The autopsy report contradicts our theory of the case, to the extent that we had one in the first place. Jacques Bisset died of natural causes, not crucifixion. The crucifixion came many hours later. We have no idea what's really going on here. Personal antipathy? A religious or political motive? There is nothing clear about this. What is clear, Chief, is that once you have Paris involved, our reputation is at stake. If Albert must be recused, who is going to solve this? We have no one on the scene. We've exonerated the archbishop, that's true, but Paris will be held to account unless we draw this case to conclusion."

"What are you suggesting?"

"I'm suggesting that I tidy things up with the last few pending cases here over the next few weeks, and then you grant me a three-month leave of absence to get to the bottom of this and win one for the team."

"Excellent!"

As I walked back into my office, the sergeant handed me the phone.

"Charles, it's Françoise."

"Hello! What a lovely surprise."

"I didn't want to bother you, but there's been another killing. A retired village priest from Saint-Alban was drowned in the fountain opposite my father's home in Béziers."

"And you think there's a connection to the crucifixion case?"

"Yes. There's been a kind of mutilation."

"I see."

"Charles, I'm scared."

"I'll make arrangements to be there this weekend. I will let you know when I arrive."

◇

After the slaughter of the First and Second World Wars, and after the influenza pandemic, the Holocaust, the explosion of the atomic bomb, and the prospect of nuclear war, a fair question might arise as to why I am so preternaturally preoccupied with the motives and methods dealing with a single homicide rather than trying to come to terms with the mass extinction of the planet. In my defense, I can only offer that there is the potential at least to understand the grand sweep of biologic cataclysm by looking through a lens at its most minute components. The most prolific of those diminutive components is, of course, the fungus.

We can be cheered up by the fact that biologists teach us that the wholesale slaughter and degradation of the planet during the twentieth century is pretty thin beer when compared to the Permian–Triassic Extinction that occurred a mere two hundred fifty million years ago. In the Great Dying, virtually all insects, 70 percent of all terrestrial vertebrates, and 96 percent of all marine life perished.

Out of this vast array of decayed organic matter emerged a clear biologic winner: fungi. Rather conveniently, the humble beetle, through its droppings, spread fungi across the entire planet. And without doubt, the noblest fungus of them all is the *Tuber melanosporum*, the black truffle. Our earliest records of human cooking describe the delicacy of truffles cooked in goose fat for the pharaohs three thousand years ago.

I think Rossini said it best when he noted that he cried only three times in his life: after his first opera failed, after hearing Paganini play the violin, and after watching a truffle-studded turkey fall overboard at a boating picnic.

As I drove the forgettable miles south to Toulouse, I could not get the vision of my first meeting with Françoise out of my mind. Her black-and-white striped blouse was, in my eyes, the perfect metaphor for the famous Lyonnais dish *poularde demi-deuil*, or chicken in half mourning. Black truffles placed beneath the skin of the chicken create alternating colors of black and white as a reflection of the half period of mourning when the widow is traditionally allowed to alternate white clothing with black. Now that I was returning to Toulouse, I felt that I was definitely returning to my white period.

One additional insight into the criminal mind that I will share at this point came to me as a boy. As soon as I was old enough to carry a picnic basket with two bottles of wine, I would go fishing before I had to go to church on Sunday mornings with my uncle Carlos. As it turns out, Uncle Carlos was in all likelihood neither my uncle nor, possibly, even named Carlos. Once, listening outside the room at a grand dinner party of my parents, I overheard my father explain to an acquaintance that Uncle Carlos was in the "extraction" business. Only in adulthood did I come to realize that what Uncle Carlos was extracting turned out to be financial support from numerous widows scattered throughout Brittany.

Uncle Carlos was a diminutive man with cornflower-blue eyes and wavy blond hair parted precisely in the middle. He was extraordinarily fastidious in his dress. In fact, I never saw Uncle

Carlos, whether at afternoon tea, fishing, or in his funeral casket, wearing anything other than a charcoal-gray three-piece suit and a high starched collar. Nimble and lithe, he was somewhat renowned as a dancer. It occurred to me years later, when one is more familiar with these things, that in retrospect Uncle Carlos may not even have been a ladies' man at all.

While not a great exemplar of Gallic probity, my uncle had, in fact, many other fascinating qualities. Chief among them was that he was an expert fly fisherman for trout. Not in the conventional sense, mind you, of someone making long, elegant casts of the fly line to see it beautifully floating across the river to the far bank. Uncle Carlos was, instead, a functional expert in trout fishing. His goal was to catch, with the utmost efficiency, the two trout that would comprise his breakfast, so he could then get on with the important business of sipping his wine in a blissful anesthetic state underneath the willows by the riverbank for the rest of a Sunday afternoon.

Usually, most fishermen, overcome with the excitement of observing a large trout break the surface of the water to gulp down a mayfly, would immediately make a cast at the same spot where the trout had risen. Uncle Carlos, however, would never make a cast until he had carefully observed multiple such rises and the intersecting surface rings that characterized the trout's feeding pattern. He would carefully note the distance traveled, the timing of the trout's rising, and the complex geometry involved.

"Never require the trout to think as you do, Charlie. Anticipate its next rising by calculating the pattern of the expanding rings. Place your fly not where the trout was, my boy, but where it will be. Be a master of anticipating the future, Charlie, and not of glorifying the past."

Of course, what Uncle Carlos was doing with his own life apart from fishing was never a pattern our family could decipher. But what he had expressed was a lofty sentiment nonetheless. Later, as a young detective in Paris, I came to appreciate the practicality of his wisdom.

While it is comforting and indeed engrossing to review the

known facts of a homicide case, in order to master the criminal mind and apprehend the criminal, one must anticipate where that mind is going next.

---◇---

> Our fleeting triumphs are like feathers in a gale. But our failures, Charlie, they are like a blind beggar rattling his tin cup beneath our windowsill who will not stop. Sometimes we must put down the newspaper, walk out onto our doorstep, and throttle the bugger.
> —A.L.

Freddy placed a great deal of stock in failure analysis. Chief among his subjects were failures of imagination, failures of precision, and something he called "satisfaction of search," or becoming so enamored by one theory of a case that one fails to see its obvious contradictions. Without any intellectual purchase on my murder investigation, I was sorely in need of rejuvenating my imagination.

Arriving late Saturday night, I was pleased to see a note from Françoise at the hotel lobby inviting me to Sunday lunch. It was wonderful to see her. I had the sense that she was relieved to see me as well. What could be more delightful than cold roast chicken, hearty onion soup, and country bread?

"How long will you be staying, Charles?"

"I've been given a three-month leave, but honestly, I will stay as long as it takes to resolve this matter."

"That's a comfort."

"Do you mind discussing some aspects of the case?"

"Not at all, though I'm not sure I can add all that much. Perhaps at some point you should speak with my father in Béziers. He grew up here. I was raised in Lyon, but after my mother died, we moved back here. This house and the house where my father and sister live were left to him when his uncle died."

"I see. What do you know about the Children's Orthopedic Hospital in Saint-Alban?"

"Very little, I'm afraid. We visited the gardens once when we first moved back. As far as I know, it seems to have a good reputation as a medical facility."

"There's some interesting history there. The children's hospital was founded by a Lady Ester Worthington, an Englishwoman, who apparently inherited the estate from her grandfather. Tell me, apart from one who is fabulously wealthy, what sort of woman founds a children's hospital and, more specifically, an orthopedic hospital?"

"Obviously someone very altruistic. Perhaps someone who was sickly as a child or perhaps had children with orthopedic problems—polio or something like that."

"There apparently were no heirs to the estate, so there are no children that we know of. Lady Worthington died just before the war. During the war, the board of directors did their best to maintain things, but in the end, the hospital was taken over by the government."

"It is a bit curious. But perhaps she just loved children, and not having any of her own, this was her way of expressing, I don't know, some sort of maternal instinct. There doesn't always have to be a sinister motive."

"No, not at all. Any thoughts on the archbishop?"

"He's a bit of a local celebrity. Rose up from a very humble background to become one of the most powerful men in the church. My father's not a fan. Says the archbishop was too close to the Vichy government and was a frequent dinner guest of Pétain."

"Interesting connection. On that note, what was the Résistance like around Toulouse?"

"I doubt it was anything like what Jean Moulin organized around Lyon. My uncle Claude from Toulouse would know more about that. He is an antique gun collector, and during the war he repaired quite a few of the rather antique rifles used by the movement. After the war there were a number of reprisals. No shortage of collaborators apparently, and those grievances still persist."

"Yes, it would be interesting for me to talk to your uncle at some point. The retired priest from Saint-Alban whose body was found in the fountain at Béziers—know anything about him?"

"Nothing really, other than what was in the paper."

I got up and placed a small log on the hearth. "And how are you holding up?"

"I'm fine, I guess. I'm just really concerned about my father. The restaurant takes up so much time that I can only be with him on my days off—Sunday and Monday."

"I understand. I hope it's some comfort to know that I've received permission for more police patrols in Béziers."

"Thank you, Charles. I just can't wake up from this nightmare. It all seems at times like some monumental accident. But these crimes—surely they can't just be an accident."

Of course, the greatest biological accident in evolutionary history led to the one of the greatest gastronomic triumphs of Lyonnais cuisine, namely, the creation of bread. Being French, the story naturally deals with sex. At the end of the last ice age some twelve thousand years ago, as the earth heated up, fortunately so did the sensuality of the wild grasses in the Levant. Primitive wheat, with its fourteen chromosomes, mated with the provocatively named goat grass with its fourteen chromosomes to produce the much plumper wild emmer wheat with twenty-eight chromosomes. The seeds of wild emmer wheat are attached to the husk in such a way that greatly enhances their propagation. But emmer was not content to be monogamous. It rather promiscuously mated with an even more attractive goat grass to produce the first bread wheat, with an impressive forty-eight chromosomes. The genius of this offspring is that the ear of the wheat is too tight to break off. While the chaff flies away with the wind, the grain conveniently falls to the ground, where it can readily be harvested.

The greatest wheat in France, of course, comes from the mountain plateaus of Auvergne with an iron-rich soil that imparts a unique texture and flavor. However, it is not just the finest wheat flour, salt, yeast, and water that are required to make the finest bread. It is also the dimension of time. Bread in Lyon requires two separate fermentations and fourteen hours of preparation. No, the official religion of Lyon is not Catholicism—it is bread.

In the eighteenth century, the average silk worker in Lyon consumed four pounds of bread a day. When the French government raised the bread prices to reduce consumption to one pound—well, why look further for the cause of the revolution?

Monday morning, I met with Sergeant Guyton as Albert was still keeping a low profile at home.

"Sergeant, no doubt you saw the dispatch from Paris placing me in charge of the investigation. I will need an office, a car, and an assistant."

"Very good, sir. I will happily serve as your assistant, sir."

"Excellent. In addition, I would like you to obtain as many of the financial records of the children's hospital as you can, both before and after the war. They must have an accounting firm that keeps all this. Let's say the last twenty years. I would also like a list of all the children staying at the hospital as patients during the years that Bisset was a patient there, as well as all Bisset's medical records. Finally, please provide me with the files on the murdered priest, along with his autopsy report. While the crucifixion might seem medieval, I would wager that the nails that were used are not. I would like a detailed analysis of them as well."

"Understood, sir."

On Sundays, Françoise would often have lunch at her house with her father and sister, and then the two of us would go for a walk along some country lane. I was most pleased when she invited her uncle Claude to lunch.

"A pleasure to meet you, Claude. Françoise has told me quite a bit about you."

"Likewise, Inspector."

"I understand you've lived in Toulouse all your life?"

"Yes, seventy-two years. Until I retired, my wife and I ran a small jewelry store in the old town."

"I understand from Françoise that you were active in the Résistance here?"

"Oh, not in the fighting. But I did repair quite a few of the rifles for the Maquis. I was good with my hands—and I collect antique guns, you see. What the Maquis had mostly was the old single-bolt Lebel 8 mm. From the Great War. Always jamming at the wrong time, apparently."

"Was there much fighting here?"

"No, not really. A few railway lines blown up, that sort of thing. Conditions changed a great deal in '42 when the SS moved in here."

"In Toulouse?"

"Yes. There was a whole Panzer division quartered here. Those men were brutal. For every German killed by the French, they would randomly kill twenty civilians."

"Were there many collaborators here?"

"Of course. Toulouse was no different from the rest of France. People did what they felt they needed to do in order to survive. It's easy now to take the moral high ground, but if you owned a small shop in 1942 and an SS officer walked in, were you not going to serve him? The bar at l'Hôtel de la Paix was, in fact, a favorite spot for the Nazi high command. All the young men in the French Army were prisoners. A great many of the women collaborated as well."

"What can you tell me about the archbishop during the war?"

"I don't follow religion very much. That's my wife's department. She actually attended his investiture in Bordeaux. A rags-to-riches success story perhaps. A lower-class boy who ascended to the highest ranks."

"I didn't realize."

"Oh yes. Started life with nothing."

"Rags to riches. How did that happen, do you suppose?"

"It's not entirely clear. Powerful allies perhaps."

"I see. Do you think he was a collaborator?"

"There were rumors, largely because of his close relationship with Pétain. The tribunal they convened after the war, though, found nothing to charge him with. There was criticism of his anti-Semitism, but that's endemic in French culture, it seems."

"Anti-Semitism?"

"Yes. One of the saddest days of my life was the day when I stood on the Pont Neuf in '42 and watched three hundred fifty of the city's finest Jewish citizens march to the station on their way to Buchenwald. I was in the jewelry business, you see, and many of them were my friends. Many of the wealthiest Jewish families went into hiding, but it seems the Nazis and local stool pigeons targeted them first and knew just where to find them. I suspect the archbishop was acquainted with many of them as well."

"Do you think he might have been implicated in their deportation?"

"There was no evidence for that at the tribunal. However, rumor has it that he has quite an art collection."

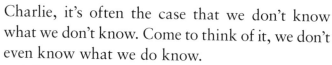

Charlie, it's often the case that we don't know what we don't know. Come to think of it, we don't even know what we do know.
—A.L.

The autopsy report of the retired priest whose mutilated body had been deposited into the main fountain in the central square came back as I had suspected. He died of natural causes; a massive cerebral infarction was detected without any evidence of head trauma. In order to move forward, I felt an acute need to have a far better understanding of the hospital, its founder, and its finances.

I felt a similarly urgent need to come to terms with the life of the archbishop. My first call was to my counterpart at Scotland Yard.

"Reggie?"

"Oh, hello, Charlie. This isn't by any chance about that five hundred quid?"

"Not at all."

"Or that Brazilian actress in my hotel room in Marseille?"

"God no, Reggie. I'm happy to say, that episode is off the radar at the moment. I just need some background information on someone, that's all. Her name is Lady Ester Worthington, the late wife of Lord Alistair Worthington. He had an estate in Sussex and was in the House of Lords."

"Worthington. I vaguely remember the name. As I recall, he was mixed up with the Mosley Blackshirt crowd."

"Lady Worthington founded a children's hospital near Toulouse, and there's something not quite right about it. I'm currently investigating several homicides, and I think there is some connection to the hospital and to her personally. I'd also be very interested in anything relevant you might dig up about His Lordship."

"Lord Worthington, right. Am I to assume this is a top priority?"

"Correct."

"And may I assume the case of Pol Roger will arrive shortly after?"

"At the conclusion, yes. And, Reggie, I want the full MI5 treatment."

My next move was to come to terms with the details of the archbishop's life and to reconcile his rise to power in the Catholic Church. Rather than raise any suspicions in the Toulouse office, I used my resources at central command in Paris. How exactly does a lower-class boy become an archbishop? Is the Catholic Church really such a meritocracy? And how had the archbishop acquired such a fabulous art collection in the process?

Part 3

When the fourteenth-century Black Plague cut its swath through Burgundy, all that the few remaining farmers could produce in bulk was the pedestrian, but low-maintenance, Gamay Beaujolais grape. Disdained in 1395 by the Duke of Burgundy as being beneath the dignity of the noble Pinot Noir, Gamay was deemed "harmful to human creatures." The consumption of Beaujolais flourished, nonetheless, downriver in gritty, working-class Lyon.

It is said that in November there are three great rivers in Lyon: the Rhône, the Saône, and Beaujolais. Every third Thursday, the Lyonnais celebrate the arrival of Beaujolais with midnight tastings at the Place des Terreaux and the Place Saint-Jean, with a citywide bacchanalia the next day. In order to make Beaujolais Nouveau, bunches of Gamay grapes must be picked by hand. Clusters of grapes are deposited whole into huge barrels with the weight of the grapes on top crushing the grapes on the bottom, releasing their juice as the intact grapes undergo fermentation. The entire process takes only six weeks, and the sooner the wine is consumed, the better. Over time, the light and fruity Beaujolais became the social lubricant for the burgeoning *bouchons* scene. Moreover, it is emblematic of the unpretentious, raucous humanity that is Lyon.

My friendship with Françoise progressed fairly well over the next few weeks. I generally felt that she looked forward to our daily meetings and was even slightly annoyed whenever I happened to be late. Moreover, I genuinely felt that more often than not she appreciated my point of view when it involved food, culture, and even politics. The curious thing was that, despite our apparent evolving closeness, even the slightest physical touch—a feeble attempt to hold her hand, for instance—seemed to put her off. As a result, I scrupulously avoided any physical contact. This seemed to put her at ease and, if anything, to enhance both her happiness and mine. While I did not understand her extreme avoidance of my touch, I have long been aware that logic does not generally apply in matters of the interaction between the sexes.

I should mention at this juncture that the failed logic of viewing homicide through the lens of rational rules could be the psychological equivalent of abstract expressionism. Intuition and gut instinct are the primary forces guiding many successful detectives such as Freddy, who was instinctively in tune with human nature. In my view, it is also important to acknowledge that there are gender differences at play here. The sad fact is that women are designed by nature to be far more sensitive and intuitive creatures. Certainly, Sandy was. Lamentably, few women choose a career as a homicide detective. The "intuition gap" I reference entails not only nonrational modes of thinking but also the recruitment of other senses and methods of sensory awareness. Curiously, I became aware of one of these extraordinary feminine traits at an early age through my discussions with Aunt Béatrice.

During my university days, I was invited to a formal dinner party at my aunt's home in Paris on rue Fontaine. At that time, she was being courted by a certain Russian émigré. It was my naive impression that the count—a worldly man, excellent conversationalist, and amiable companion—might not be a bad match for my widowed aunt. At the end of the evening when all the guests had departed, I remember distinctly my aunt Béatrice delivering this rather poignant soliloquy:

"Since early childhood, I have trusted my sense of smell to a far greater extent than all other senses. I have looked into this matter quite extensively, Charles, and leading experts in brain research have recently confirmed what I have intuitively known since childhood: that the origin of our sense of smell comes from somewhere deep within a very primitive portion of our brains. This area, as cleverly directed by God and human evolution, is apparently unencumbered by the manipulation of higher cerebral control. I can honestly say that, for me, the scent of another person has always been a direct, unambiguous, and informative insight into said person's character. I can share with you, Charles, that I have, on more than one occasion, been sorely deceived by the sight, the sound, or, yes, even the touch of another, either male or female. Yet for me, no amount of artificial fragrance can obscure the smell of dishonesty, hypocrisy, feigned sincerity, or for that matter, true love. Nature has quite cleverly simplified matters by rendering most men virtual novices when it comes to smell. It has been my observation, Charles, that men such as the count have overcompensated for this deficit by acquiring an acute sixth sense. And that is an overarching sense of their self-importance."

◇

James Joyce, while masquerading as a novelist, was the greatest linguist of the twentieth century. His brother Stanislas, however, was the superior philosopher. It was Stanislas's observation that friendship among men was impossible because there could be no sex and that friendship between men and women was impossible because there must be sex.

◇

Our relationship changed a great deal in early April, when Françoise's father, Arthur, was admitted to the hospital in Béziers with pneumonia. He had visibly become frailer than when I met him in early February. Françoise was right to be worried. We immediately set about a plan to provide a constant vigil for Arthur at the hospital.

After the hotel kitchen had closed for the night, I would drive Françoise to the hospital in Béziers so she could spend the night on a cot next to her father's bed there. I would pick her up at the hospital at 4:30 a.m. and then drive her to Toulouse so we could have breakfast together at the central market. After she had shopped for the hotel's food, I would drive her back to my room at the hotel to rest. I moved my base of operations from Toulouse to the police department in Béziers so that every few hours I could look in on Arthur and phone Françoise about his progress. After work I would stay at the hospital until Françoise was done in the kitchen. Then I would once again pick her up. We would repeat this round-the-clock schedule the next day.

Fortunately, Arthur responded to the product of another great fungus, penicillin, and after a fortnight, he miraculously turned the corner.

That evening we celebrated Arthur's remarkable, if improbable, recovery with a glass of champagne in my hotel room. There is scant explanation for what next transpired after we finished the bottle.

"Charles, put down your glass. Look at me, Charles. I am a woman. I want you to make love to me."

Charlie, when it comes to men understanding women, the term *idiot savant* comes to mind. Or perhaps only the first half of the equation.
—A.L.

The Romans knew a good piece of real estate when they saw one. Situated on a hill overlooking the confluence of the Rhône and Saône, the Roman city of Lyon, or Lugdunum, quite literally means "fortress on a hill." The city became a thriving commercial center as the provincial capital and a key military outpost in the Roman struggle against the Germanic tribes. To ensure the safety of the city, the Romans built no fewer than four separate aqueducts into Lyon, supplying water for a population that had reached two hundred thousand by AD 200.

From the outset, the populace of Lyon exhibited none of the feigned superiority of Paris or Bordeaux. Indeed, the enduring cultural legacy of the city of Lyon was one of generosity and tolerance that can best be seen in its response to the emperor Nero. Though Nero was despised throughout the empire as an extraordinarily venal and cruel man, the Lyonnais had a unique trait of seeing some good in everyone. After the devastation of the Great Fire of Rome in AD 64, it was the Lyonnais who contributed four million sesterces to Nero's coffers for the rebuilding of the Eternal City. Several years later, after Lyon itself was leveled by fire, Nero returned the favor with an equal sum of money.

Arthur's illness coincided with a dearth of new information about the case, as I had yet to hear back from either Reggie or Paris. I used the resultant lull to catch up with Oscar and Emma. Given the peculiarities of the case, I was particularly keen to gain some of Emma's historical insight into the Languedoc, which might provide additional context. Emma suggested we have lunch at a café in Béziers near the central square.

I waited until after our meal to begin my inquiry by producing a black-and-white forensic photograph of the cross, fortunately without the victim.

"Emma, as a medieval historian, does anything strike you as unusual about the cross used in this crucifixion?"

"Well, it's a Cathar cross. Quite typical with the curving along the edges here. There are very popular replicas in the tourist shops in Toulouse. There's been a resurgence of interest in the Cathars since the war. You can go on tours to see their beautiful ruined castles in the area."

"Forgive my ignorance, but who were the Cathars?"

"They were a medieval religious sect spread throughout much of the Languedoc. Quite a large group, actually, who absolutely rejected the authority and wealth of the Catholic Church in Rome and all its sacraments and rituals. They tried to lead very pure lives, and their goal was to lead such a humble and ascetic existence that they would be chosen as one of the perfecti. That way they could escape the cycle of rebirth. I like to think of them as medieval Buddhists."

"Remarkable. Did the Cathars themselves think of their religion as being Christian?"

"In some ways, yes. They saw themselves as followers of the true principles of Christianity—of poverty, simplicity, and loving one's neighbor. But it might be fair to say they were primarily dualists who saw the material world as evil and the spiritual world as good. That is why they rejected the divinity of the man Jesus, because he was of the material world and must have therefore been evil."

"How did the Catholic Church react to that concept?"

"With horror. Most people don't realize that the First Crusade authorized by the pope was not against Muslims but against apostate Christians, the Cathars. In 1209, Pope Innocent III sent a massive army to subdue the Cathars. Right here in the town of Béziers, the Crusaders slaughtered seven thousand men, women, and children. There were perhaps only two hundred Cathars living in the town at that point, but the town fathers refused to give them up. The papal legate overseeing the assault callously ordered the soldiers to indiscriminately kill every single one of the townsfolk, famously saying, 'God will recognize his own.'"

"How remarkable. Are there still Cathars, or has that sect gone completely extinct?"

"Oh no, it's still with us. Not in the public eye, given the authority of the church, but there are still active pockets. It might interest you to know that the Duke d'Antoigne, who originally built the estate in Saint-Alban, was a very prominent Cathar perfecti. Many of his workers there were also presumed to be Cathars."

"How interesting."

"Ironic, isn't it, Charles, because the perfecti famously abhorred sex. They were strict vegetarians because they could not bring themselves to eat any animal that reproduced by way of sexual intercourse. That is what eventually brought about the sale of the d'Antoigne estate. He, of course, never married and had no heirs."

"That's quite a story. One last question, Emma. What do you make of this photo of the hand ax that was found in the victim's skull? I thought the medieval French fought with swords and pikes."

"That's correct. It's not a French weapon—or even an English weapon for that matter. That ax is a replica of a medieval Dane ax used by the Vikings."

"Amazing. What's its modern significance, do you think?"

"They were collected by the Nazis, who prized them for their connection to the Vikings. In the minds of the SS, the Vikings were the original Aryans."

The term *berserk* comes from a description of the tenth-century Viking warriors who were the personal bodyguards to the Byzantine emperor in Constantinople. These Norsemen fought completely covered in animal skins while wielding the Dane ax. They were referred to as "berserkers" because they went into battle channeling their "animal" strength in a howling, frenzied trance.

Before I knew it to be the site of a Cathar massacre, the town of Béziers held a special meaning for me. It was the birthplace of Jean Moulin. There were, in my opinion, a number of genuine heroes of the French Résistance, but few who were lawyers—nevertheless, Moulin was just such a hero. It was perhaps inevitable that he would set up his base of operations in Lyon with its ethos of rebellion. There he coordinated and cajoled the warring factions of Résistance fighters.

Moulin's favorite place to hold Résistance meetings under the nose of the SS was the *bouchon* Le Garet, where the pike dumplings in crayfish sauce were each the size of a grapefruit. White lace curtains on its front door and windows offered the advantage of allowing waiters to readily observe Nazis on the street, whereas the Germans were unable to look into the restaurant and were repelled by its redolence of courage.

London finally called the next morning.

"Lady Worthington," Reggie reported, "was not at all the posh type you might think. Daughter of a baker from Leeds named Maguire. Grammar school education, then went to work for Lord Worthington at his estate in Sussex as a governess for his daughter. Seems the old boy took a fancy to her. Worked there a couple of years. Then she goes away to a sort of finishing school in Switzerland for a year. The old man pays for it. His Lordship soon thereafter ditches his wife, and when Ester comes back, he up and marries her."

"What do you know about that year she spent alone in Switzerland? That's a bit odd for a governess."

"Right, a bit odd, that. Nothing in the files though. You'll have to sort that one out on your own."

"What about children? Any of her own?"

"None apparently. His Lordship's daughter from his first marriage died in a boating accident as a teenager off the Isle of Wight. So, no heirs. And the estate was passed on to his nephew when His Lordship kicked the bucket. Took a few years, but the nephew managed to blow through all the fortune he had inherited with bogus investment schemes after the war. Oh, and there was a lot of bad blood between His Lordship and his brother Edward. Seems there were multiple lawsuits filed against Edward for embezzling family funds."

"Anything surface on the children's hospital?"

"It seems that while the Lord was spending his money on Oswald Mosley's Blackshirt crowd, Lady Worthington put a small fortune into that place in Toulouse."

One good hunch, Charlie, is worth a dozen so-called facts.
—A.L.

There are times in the investigation of a complex murder case when one must abandon the siren song of reason and follow one's instincts. My thoughts turned to the olfactory insights of Aunt Béatrice. The entire situation with Ester Maguire exuded an aroma of incongruity. I know the English aristocracy well enough to know that they would no sooner pay a governess an extra shilling for a superlative job than they would eat well-done roast beef. A lavish year in a Swiss finishing school was too tantalizing a cultural discrepancy to pass up, so the next morning I found myself on the train to Geneva.

As part of my English birthright, I am congenitally accustomed to queuing in line and coping patiently with the delays and obfuscations offered up by minor functionaries of a determined, self-gratulatory bureaucracy. I attribute this predisposition to vestigial remnants of Europe's Victorian upper classes clinging to an illusion of protocol as a protest against the general erosion of cultural standards resulting from the ascendancy of the middle classes. However, the labyrinthine morass of futile interactions I encountered at the Gustav International School for Girls in Verbier, Switzerland, transcended the realm of Dickens and catapulted me into a truly Orwellian sphere.

Remember, Charlie, the donkey with the heaviest burden kicks up the most dust.
—A.L.

The girls' school with its Romanesque facade, Corinthian columns, ostentatious marble staircases, and huge arrangements of fresh flowers was housed in a very impressive building, in a very Swiss sort of way. It was mostly empty. Its long, empty corridors suggested a gradual and forlorn descent from a glorious past. Its practical but imperial splendor seemed a cross between a faux Versailles and a Medici bank.

In separate conversations with the registrar, the dean of students, the bursar, the head of the school, and the legal counsel, all I could ascertain was that there was very possibly a student named Ester Maguire who had very likely attended school there in 1887 or 1888. What she studied, the degree she obtained, or any details of her time there must have been recorded by Hammurabi.

A lesson I learned in the army is that in dealing with a hierarchical institution, there is an inverse relationship between the truth and one's rank. I was eager, therefore, to interview the little people: clerical staff, maids, cooks, servants, even other students who might have known Ester. Given the famous longevity of the Swiss, who stubbornly refuse to indulge in any pleasurable mode of human existence that might be harmful to health, there was a chance that at least some of those people still existed.

After more fruitless rounds with the polite, reserved, and unhelpful school officials, I found myself wandering along a succession of empty corridors in search of the origin of a distinct odor of brass polish. The source of that scent was an ancient-looking cleaning woman doing battle with a never-ending staircase railing. She seemed quite happy to strike up a conversation with me.

"A student in 1887, you said? A long time ago, monsieur. Before the war. Now those were the days, monsieur. All the girls in their long ball gowns. The dancing and the parties. Even their servants looking smart in their finery."

I quickly looked through the file I was holding. The bursar had, in fact, recorded a boarding fee for a servant, a Madame Margaret Jones. Again, it struck me as odd that a governess would be traveling with a servant.

"Did the girls take classes here apart from the balls?"

"Many girls did. Or, rather, some did. Some, not all. Perhaps a bit of French. A bit of geography perhaps. Lots of skiing."

"And the girls who did not take classes, I take it that their time here was a sort of finishing school to learn the social graces?"

"You could say that, monsieur. There were other benefits to the school for the young ladies. Back then it was different, you see."

"The trouble is, madame, I am here in an official capacity for the French Justice Ministry, and there seem to be very few records for this young lady. Why would that be the case, do you suppose?"

The elderly woman visibly blushed and then leaned her head toward my ear and spoke softly, "Perhaps, monsieur, you should look for her records at the maternity hospital. It was a different time then, a different school, monsieur."

Having dealt with a number of hospital clerks over the years, I know that they are a consistent and, dare I say, admirable lot. In my experience, they are relatively immune to the sorts of bribery and flattery one typically dispenses. They are much more akin to military personnel and respond most readily to a chain-of-command approach. After a heavy dose of impressive-looking credentials from the Justice Ministry in Paris, the middle-aged clerk with a clipped mustache and thinning hair was more than willing to plow through back records at the Verbier Lying-in Hospital. I was counting on the fact that no one keeps more fastidious records than the Swiss, even if they do speak French.

The clerk lifted up his wire-rimmed glasses to peer at the paperwork. "You say an Englishwoman? Age approximately nineteen or twenty? During the years 1887 and 1888? Name of Maguire?"

"Correct."

"I am sorry, Inspector. We have a detailed list of all foreign nationals admitted for childbirth during those years, and her name is not on that list—even going back to 1886."

"I see. Were there any Englishwomen at all admitted during that time interval?"

"Let me see. Only one, Inspector. In February of 1888 there was a Jones."

"Would that possibly be a Madame Margaret Jones?"

"That is correct, sir."

"And the birth was recorded as a live birth?"

"I can see from our records in 1888 that she gave birth to twin boys on February 16. There are several notes in the discharge summary, however, Inspector. The first is a note from the midwife that one child was born with a clubfoot. The second is that Madame Jones had a prolonged admission to the hospital. For peritonitis, it seems. That year, 1888, was a calamitous one. That was the year of the great avalanche. The town suffered greatly."

There can be no great cuisine without suffering, and Lyon is no exception to this rule. At the dawn of the Industrial Revolution, the production of high-quality silk made Lyon enormously prosperous. The town became the envy of the rest of France. Under appalling conditions, thousands of the city's *canuts* toiled day and night at their massive looms. By 1834, the demand for silk in England spurred a surge of exports and enriched factory owners. Despite their newfound wealth, merchants who bought and sold the silk greedily sought to cut payment to the *canuts*. On April 9 of that year, six thousand of them revolted, rapidly taking over all the main government buildings. The army abandoned Lyon, only to reappear, massively reinforced, to bombard the city. Six hundred were killed in the retaking of Lyon and the suppression of the revolt. It must be said, however, that the egalitarian spirit of the *canuts* inspired the citizens of Lyon and has played its part in producing a distinctive gastronomy for the workingman.

Françoise and I had just finished our cognac in the hotel library. I reached inside my pocket for the car keys. It was nearly eleven on a Saturday night, and I was greatly looking forward to a deliciously sound sleep and then a bracing full cooked breakfast at her house.

"Let's just stay a bit longer, Charles, and enjoy the silence."

A clear signal that there will be no silence, only a series of dramatic pauses.

"Of course."

"There is something I've been meaning to talk to you about, Charles, and I just never seem to find the right time."

There is never a good time to talk about these things because the chance of effective communication between the sexes is approximately the same as my chances of swimming the English Channel in half an hour.

"Is now a good time?"

Now is not a good time because my mental capacity at the moment is so highly compromised by fatigue and alcohol that it is very unlikely that I will sufficiently parry the thrust to make any remotely adequate response to prevent my emotional three-masted clipper ship from crashing onto the rocks of feminine disapproval.

"Of course. What's on your mind, dear?"

"Charles, one of the things that I enjoy most about our relationship is our openness and honesty. I feel that I can honestly say anything and everything on my mind."

Never were spoken truer words.

"I would hope so."

"Of course, there are times when you do things that annoy me.

Rather frequently, in fact. And I always have had the freedom to point those things out to you. But you never seem to complain all that much. So, I want you to be totally honest with me, Charles. What single thing do I do that annoys you the most? Be honest now."

I have presented the state's evidence at a Supreme Court inquiry against a former justice minister involving the death of his mistress. Somehow, I feel that the stakes are higher in this particular court of law.

"If you really must know—and I'm very sorry to bring this up, but I will do so since you asked—I get quite annoyed when I tell you that we have just five minutes to go before we must leave for the restaurant, then you just throw something on in a mad dash and somehow manage to look as ravishing as Cleopatra."

There is no way to predict the outcome of these conversations. The best one can hope for is a Pyrrhic victory that allows for a more orderly retreat.

At this point, the only way to describe the Saint-Alban case was to liken it to a pointillist painting by Seurat with single dots dispersed among four corners. On my return from Verbier, I talked the situation over at length with Françoise. We agreed that I desperately needed to speak with individuals old enough to have direct personal knowledge of Lady Worthington, Bisset, and the archbishop.

I also felt that it was curious that I had not spoken in any detail with Albert about the case. Of course, there was the issue of his recusal, and then the birth of his grandson, but I found it odd that we had not spoken in a more formal way about the investigation. I was eager to know more about the financial dealings of his father and the archbishop that had prompted Albert's recusal.

I knew that Marcel Dumont, Albert's father, not only had inherited great wealth but also had greatly expanded it by building the largest Renault factory in the South of France. He had been under investigation in the twenties and then later in the thirties for lavish donations to the Catholic Church and various right-wing

71

political groups organized to suppress the Communist-led labor movement. What I hadn't realized was his sub-rosa connection to the Dreyfus affair.

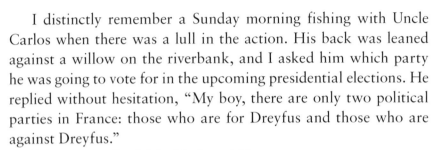

I distinctly remember a Sunday morning fishing with Uncle Carlos when there was a lull in the action. His back was leaned against a willow on the riverbank, and I asked him which party he was going to vote for in the upcoming presidential elections. He replied without hesitation, "My boy, there are only two political parties in France: those who are for Dreyfus and those who are against Dreyfus."

I do not recall which side he said he was on.

There can be no doubt that the foundational influences on the French psyche, and hence French culture and cuisine, include Charlemagne, the French Revolution, Napoleon, and the Dreyfus affair—but not necessarily in that order. Although Charlemagne promulgated laws that ensured tolerance for Jews, French kings throughout the Middle Ages vacillated between persecution and expulsion, with reinstatement only whenever it was in their financial interests to borrow money from Jewish people. Edicts from the French Revolution and, later, from Napoleon finally freed Jews from overt political persecution, but they did not eliminate a deeply entrenched French anti-Semitism.

In 1894 a French artillery officer, Alfred Dreyfus, was wrongfully convicted of sharing military secrets with the Germans. As a result, he spent five years in the penal colony of Devil's Island. When it became clear that the evidence against Dreyfus was fraudulent, he was recalled to France and retried. Remarkably, evidence at that trial was also tainted, and he was once again convicted. New documents, however, soon came to light, and Dreyfus was ultimately pardoned and reinstated as a military officer.

The Dreyfus affair exposed deep fault lines just beneath the thin crust of the egalitarian French society. On one hand were Dreyfus's defenders, the anticlerical Dreyfusards, who represented the ideals of the Revolution; on the other, the elite, conservative forces in French society embodied by the Catholic Church and the army officer class.

———◇———

I needed to finally have that meeting with Albert, so I arranged to meet him at his office the following morning.

There is nothing normal about the École normale supérieure, but it certainly perceives itself as being superior. Imagine if Oxford, Cambridge, and Harvard were combined into a flavorless academic cassoulet dedicated solely to the production of a humorless intellectual class destined for the upper echelons of the soul-crushing French professional bureaucracy. Oscar and I would speak of its graduates as the "goldies," a reference to both the oversized goldfish pond commanding the school's central courtyard and the main source of the alumni's personal motivation.

Albert was indeed a goldie. His academic pedigree, plus a seemingly inexhaustible wellspring of family money, ensured a rapid ascent through the ranks at the Ministry of Justice. Though five years younger, he was now technically my superior. We had both spent time in the Central Bureau in Paris. To be fair, I had always enjoyed my interactions with Albert since he seemed aware of the many advantages life held in store for him. I met with him in his office to gently probe what he knew that I didn't about the archbishop.

He began in a very forthright manner: "Look, Charlie, I know it might seem that I've been avoiding you, but in reality, there have been quite a few distractions."

"I understand. I've been preoccupied with a number of things as well, but it's good that we have the time now. If you don't mind, I want to begin with the most difficult question first."

"Certainly."

"Tell me why you felt you had to recuse yourself."

"I'm going to be completely honest with you about this. When I first heard about the murder—the crucifixion—and that this might involve the archbishop even in a tangential way, I called the Central Bureau and asked to be let off the case. To be clear, I requested this. But let me give you a little additional background. My late father, Marcel, funded a number of right-wing causes. I'm not personally sympathetic to that point of view, but the fact remains that he did this, even as a young man."

"I do remember reading that he bankrolled that anti-Dreyfus newspaper."

"Yes, *La Libre Parole*. And my father could never accept the fact that Dreyfus was exonerated. It just enraged him. As a consequence, he started financially backing other right-wing political groups, as well as the military and the Catholic Church. In the twenties he became very fearful of the Communist Party, especially when he saw them take hold in places such as Lyon and Toulouse. At that point he started backing the then bishop of Toulouse, Father Loriot, to become archbishop."

"As a move against the Communists?"

"Yes. Remember, there were several strikes at his Renault plants organized by the left, and he saw them as a threat. He viewed Fabien Loriot as an ally in that struggle."

"Tell me about your father's collaboration with Vichy and the Nazis."

"Look, it all came out in the tribunal after the war. There's nothing to hide here. There's no denying the fact that Renault manufactured over thirty thousand vehicles for the Germans. That's why the British bombed their factories in 1944. Of course, what my father said in his defense was that he had saved thousands of French car workers from being exported as slave labor to the Reich."

"And what about the relationship between your father, the archbishop, and Pétain?"

"There's no question they were close friends. I remember as a teenager seeing the three of them at our house for Sunday dinner."

"How did your father's money help support the archbishop?"

"Well, for one thing, when the archbishop's original summer residence burned down, I believe it was in 1928 or '29, my father paid quite a sum to have it rebuilt."

"And the archbishop's rather extravagant art collection?"

"I honestly don't know much about it. I've only seen it once. From what I remember, I'll admit it is remarkable. Here's what I know and what I don't know. My father had several secret warehouses, mostly in the mountains. I know that he stored his own art collection there, as he knew Goering was obsessed with old masters. Look, I can tell you that my father, despite the anti-Semitism of his youth, had several wealthy Jewish business partners. What is rumored, but what I can't confirm, is that he stored their art collections there for safekeeping as well."

"Those business partners ... is it true they were all sent to Buchenwald?"

"I believe so, yes. But please, Charles, I ask you to see my father's actions in light of his passion against communism and as an attempt to preserve our way of life. You have to understand that France could have gone communist."

Ho Chi Minh, the Vietnamese freedom fighter, was a founding member of the French Communist Party in 1920. It is one of the great ironies of history that the entire course of events in Southeast Asia might have turned out to be completely different if his application for a position as a lowly clerk in the French Colonial Administrative School had not been repeatedly denied.

One Sunday afternoon after lunch as I was tidying up, Françoise asked me in a rather casual, random way, "Charles, what do you think about children?"

In reality, I have few thoughts on this subject.

Fortunately, my years of intense legal training kicked in. I responded appropriately, if tentatively, while trying desperately not to drop the soup terrine, "Why? What do you think about children?"

"I don't know. Perhaps I'm too old, but somehow I can't imagine a life without them." I said nothing, but she pressed on. "Do you think you'd make a good father?"

Not surprisingly, I have even fewer thoughts on this subject.

Mercifully, the terrine was resting firmly on the shelf at this point. For some reason my mind transported me back to my childhood and the many humid, languid afternoons along the Seine accompanying an inebriated and snoring Uncle Carlos.

"Actually, I think so, yes. I believe I know exactly what not to do."

In an effort to better understand the local political climate, that Monday afternoon I decided to take a drive and have a chat with the mayor of Saint-Alban, Monsieur Gerard Norvelle. We had a glass of wine at the village café in the central square.

"Monsieur le Mayor, I must admit how impressed I am by how prosperous your community seems to be."

"Well, there was relatively little fighting here, so reconstruction was much easier."

"I noticed quite a few new homes along the river—some even under construction."

"After the war, much of the hospital's land along the river was sold off to pay for debts and to modernize the hospital. There were a number of individuals from the village and as far away as Bordeaux and Paris who bought up the lands. So, it was a small real estate boom. It has since quieted down. Saint-Alban has its charms, but sadly there is no Opéra."

"Tell me, what is the villager's view of the archbishop?"

"In general, it's quite positive. He has always been a presence in the community. We are honored to have him here."

The mayor was a man of my age, so I decided to ask him about his experience in the war.

"Tell me, Monsieur le Mayor, what was it like here in Saint-Alban during the war?"

He swirled his glass for a moment. "I wouldn't know. I was a prisoner of war in Germany."

"Well, we share that in common. At least for a year and a half."

The mayor leaned back in his chair in a rather defensive way. "Really? I would have thought someone from your background would have found a backdoor out of that hellhole."

"My background and my war experience are not that remarkable or even that important. What is important is what happened at the children's hospital and to the residents of Saint-Alban during the war."

"But perhaps your war experience is important, Inspector. Perhaps it might be difficult for you to understand what went on here."

"Well, to be brief, I escaped to London. After a time with the Free French, I joined the British Army and fought in North Africa."

"Gin and tonic at the officers' club then?"

"Our evenings were more often preoccupied with doings things such as crawling through minefields to capture SS colonels."

Just then, the waiter, whom I had previously noted standing idly at the bar, came forward with a cheese plate as if to break up the tension.

"Compliments of the house, monsieur."

"Ah, the famous Saint-Alban goat cheese. Merci."

At that point the mayor folded his arms.

"Since I wasn't here during the war, I doubt that I will be of much use to you."

The mayor got up to leave, but then suddenly he turned around and offered, "We can't all be heroes, Inspector."

During my years in the army, I did encounter a few truly courageous individuals one might refer to as heroes. Certainly, what Oscar did with his chess match in the prison camp qualifies him for the title. For those on the civilian front faced with the plague of Nazi occupation for five years, I'm inclined to agree with Camus's definition of heroism. For Camus, a hero is just an ordinary man or woman who does extraordinary things in the face of evil merely out of a profound sense of decency.

It is not for me to judge the citizens of France during the occupation. The war was an unfathomable tragedy for everyone on so many levels that it defies simple categorizations of guilt or innocence.

Even in peacetime, human interactions are so fraught with peril that we must cherish the few moments in our lives when things appear to go well.

Charlie, my boy, if by some miracle you ever find the right woman, act quickly before she changes her mind.
—A.L.

After dinner, Françoise began in a plaintive voice, "Charles, how soon is this case likely to end?"

"I have no idea."

"I don't want it to end. When it ends, you'll have to go back to Paris, and then I'll have no one to argue with over how best to prepare root vegetables."

"In that case, I'm certain it will last a very, very long time."

The next morning, sitting outside my office was a thin, anxious man in an ill-fitting blue serge suit. He nervously twirled the hat in his hand. It was the waiter from the village café in Saint-Alban. I ushered him in.

"Thank you for seeing me, Inspector. My name is Vignot. Robert Vignot."

"Yes, from the café. Please have a seat, Monsieur Vignot."

"I wanted to tell you that what the mayor said to you is not true. Well, at least not entirely. It's not the whole story. Not even his own history. Yes, he was indeed a prisoner of war in Germany, but he got out early. In '44. There were rumors that bribes were paid through Vichy officials to get him released after a year. And the money came from the archbishop. You see, my wife worked at the children's hospital for a while during the war as a secretary to the head doctor, a Dr. Villmont. She overheard the archbishop bragging about it to him."

"I see. And why would the archbishop do that? Pay bribes for the mayor's release?"

"I don't know. I've wondered that myself. My wife told me that terrible things were going on at the hospital before she died in '45."

"Terrible things?"

"Yes, but she was always too ashamed to tell me. She quit after working there for a year."

"I see."

"There was a lot of money floating around the hospital, Inspector. There were lavish parties with German officers and the archbishop. Villmont himself was a Nazi sympathizer. He left right after the Americans came and before the Maquis could get him. I believe he committed suicide. Inspector, I am telling you that there was a lot of money there."

◇

Money is not the root of all evil, Charlie. Never forget, it's also the tree trunk, the branches, the twigs, and the leaves.
—A.L.

The following morning, I finally received several large manila envelopes containing copies of the hospital's financial records going back some twenty years. It has always been my observation that institutional financial statements come in two broad categories: either a fiduciary Potemkin village or a hall of mirrors. The only reliable way to unravel this monetary Gordian knot was to enlist the aid of the criminals whose profession it is to falsify them.

One such criminal was Camille "Candy" Bergeron, currently doing a life sentence in a Marseille prison for embezzling millions from the pension funds of war widows. Candy had murdered his partner who had exposed his financial crime, and Freddy and I had had the pleasure of obtaining his conviction. It was a short train ride to Marseille and worth a roll of the dice.

Even in his sixties and garbed in an ill-fitting black-and-white-striped prison uniform, Candy had his dyed red hair perfectly parted on the side and his beard neatly trimmed to expose a faint hint of matching rouge. He had a habit in the courtroom of holding his hands together at the fingertips as if in prayer. His character, however, was far from angelic.

"What's in this for me, Inspector? It's not as if doing this little job for you is going to gain my release."

"That is correct. Think of it this way, Candy—when the righteous fling open the gates of hell, let's hope they push your cage back a bit from the eternal flames."

He said nothing, only tapped his fingertips to an unheard rhythm in his head.

"There are other factors to consider, Candy. Over the years, perhaps a more bracing climate, say, near Brittany or Normandy, might be a bit healthier and a bit more invigorating than the sweltering summers here in Marseille. I also hear from your custodians that you're not a particularly popular dinner guest among the Algerian clientele at their intimate soirées."

"The salt air of Normandy has a certain appeal. What is it you want exactly?"

"I'm investigating a homicide outside of Toulouse."

"The crucifixion involving the archbishop?"

"Yes."

"Interesting religious symbolism, but not my style, Inspector. You'll recall, I much prefer quietly stealing my money and then delivering the more humane denouement of a bullet to the head."

"What I want is for you to examine the financial records of a private children's hospital where the victim spent his childhood. The archbishop was also involved, with the hospital and its founder, a Lady Worthington. I want you to see if there's any financial connection, any source leading to a financial motive to commit this crime. The archbishop's current financial position seems out of proportion to his ecclesiastical status."

"Didn't take the vow of poverty? Well, few do."

"He has an extensive art collection."

"I see. A private children's hospital. A gold mine for someone in my line of work. Easy to muddy the waters and mix up charitable donations with endowment, investment income, and operational funds. A few thousand here, a few thousand there, and no one's the wiser."

"I figured you'd have some experience with this."

"Oh yes. I should point out that a chartered private hospital has a tax-exempt status. However, the hospital still must have its board of trustees file a certified annual financial statement."

I handed over the bulky packet. "There are quite a few documents here—annual statements, bank receipts, that sort of thing. When do you think you might have something for me?"

"My dance card looks quite empty at the moment, Inspector. I will need a private room and a telephone with an outside line—for professional inquiries, mind you."

"Agreed."

"I think in a week I will know at least if someone is massaging the books. Who knows, Inspector, perhaps instead of couscous I'll someday soon be dining on—"

"Lobster Thermidor?"

On my return from Marseille, I placed a phone call to the archbishop as a follow-up to my conversation with Albert.

"Of course, it's true, Inspector. Marcel Dumont was a devout Catholic and donated generously to the church. You must understand the difficult political times in the thirties, Inspector. With labor strikes and unrest, the church was the only bulwark against the communists, who were taking over the government. And, yes, when the summer residence burned down, he was very helpful in raising funds to rebuild it. My financial relationship with Marcel all came out in the tribunal. And, no, it is not true at all that any of my artwork is from Jews killed in the Holocaust. That is absurd. I have an entirely different aesthetic."

An antidote to my unsatisfying conversation with the archbishop was supplied by Sergeant Guyton, who presented me with a detained biographical file on the dead priest found in Béziers, Émile Lauron.

"Seems, sir, he was convicted of collaboration in 1946 by the regional tribunal. Spent two years in jail. Was defrocked. One witness at the trial testified that Father Émile revealed to the SS the hiding places of several prominent Jewish families in Toulouse."

"I see. Sergeant, could you look in the files and see if we have anything on a Dr. Villmont, who was the medical director of the children's hospital during the war? A final, if unconventional, request, Sergeant: I would like x-rays taken in the morgue of both Jacque Bisset's feet."

"X-rays. The feet. Very good, sir."

The next Sunday morning after breakfast, the weather was delightful, so Françoise and I went for a leisurely walk along the Tarn River.

"Charles, do you consider yourself a good Catholic?"

I must somehow manage to thread the needle in between Marxist atheism and Opus Dei.

"I would say my love for the church is primarily mediated through my love for its Christmas music."

Sincere, if deliberately vague.

"But you know what I mean."

"Yes, but I'm more inclined to agree with Voltaire, that we'd better be content to make the world we live in our earthly paradise."

"But you'd have no objection to my beliefs as a Catholic?"

"I would adhere to the Lateran Council of 1215, if that would make you happy."

The Lateran Council ordered a four-year truce among Christians not for the sake of peace, but in order to launch a new Crusade to the Holy Land.

"But why are you still a skeptic about all the miracles? Aren't they inspiring?"

"Impressive, no doubt."

It would not be useful at this that point to comment on the irrationality of religion or to say that to Voltaire, the only inspiring miracle was human consciousness.

In 1911 Freud published an essay analyzing the psychotic delusions of a previously respected German appellate judge, Dr. Daniel Schreber, who had been institutionalized for schizophrenia. Freud focused on the psychodynamics of Schreber's desire to transform his body into that of a female in order to mate with God through "divine rays," populate the world, and then become the Redeemer of the universe.

To Freud, it seemed that Schreber was essentially creating a new religion. He wondered what would happen if future generations were to find more truth in Schreber's delusions than in Freud's sober analysis. What if masses of people ultimately became converts to Schreber's fantasies and began to worship him as a "Christlike" redeemer? After all, what difference was there between Schreber's irrational stories and the Christian belief that Jesus rose from the dead, or that Muhammad ascended into heaven on a winged horse? More to the point, was the crucifixion in Saint-Alban perpetrated by a blindly fanatical religious zealot or a clear-eyed man who knew precisely the psychological effect it would create?

I was still waiting for news from Paris, so I decided to arrange a visit with the Kunstels and take them up on their invitation to see the hospital library to gain some insight into the early history of the place. Perhaps there might be some people still alive who knew Her Ladyship.

As I drove along the back roads in early spring, exploring the river valley leading up to Saint-Alban, I was struck by the verdant natural beauty of the scenery along the Tarn River with the many prosperous farms dotted along its banks.

"Good afternoon, Inspector. I'm not sure if you've met my husband, Peter."

Peter was a short, muscular man with small wire-rimmed glasses. His face was leathery, having been reddened by the sun. His chapeau was tilted to the side of his bald head.

"A pleasure. I understand you are the expert who tends the marvelous gardens. It must be quite an operation."

"It is. I mostly oversee the crew. But I'm hardly qualified to be an expert. Sort of a jack-of-all-trades, you might say. I oversee the tree trimming, the repair shop for heavy equipment, and the carpentry shop for all the trellises. Monsieur de Silva, he was the real expert."

"Monsieur de Silva was the original designer of the gardens?"

"That's correct. He passed away shortly after the war, but he left detailed instructions for all the maintenance."

"I understand you moved here from Holland in the thirties?"

"Yes. Ada has chronic bronchitis. The climate is so much better here for her."

"Of course. Well, I wonder if I might first visit the library that you mentioned last time? To get a better sense of the history of the place."

The library was a charming sunlit room jutting out from the main hospital corridor just beyond the foyer.

"Tell me about these lovely prints and some of these pictures."

"Along this wall there are prints of the original plans for the gardens, and here you can see Her Ladyship walking the grounds with Monsieur de Silva with his workmen from Italy. They had to import quite a few plants from Tuscany. Notice this picture of the natural spring on the side of the hill here. They created an extensive irrigation system that minimizes the amount of water needed for all the trees and shrubs. Quite modern for its day."

"I see. And what are these paintings along this wall?"

"Those were part of Her Ladyship's personal art collection. There are paintings all over the hospital, even on the wards. Here are some of her favorite still life oils of flowers."

"Beautiful."

"From what I understand, many were purchased for her by Monsieur de Silva. He was not only a landscape architect but also a very accomplished art dealer."

"Really? Some of the frames are quite new. Quite beautiful, but new."

"Interesting that you noticed that. Peter is quite proud of restoring some of these. Woodworking is his hobby."

"Very intricate and ornate detail, Peter. Lovely."

"Thank you, Inspector. It's an honor for me to create these beautiful frames in my little workshop."

"Well, I wonder if you might point me in the direction of someone still living in the area from the early days of the hospital? I recognize this was some time ago, but are there any staff or, perhaps, any of Lady Worthington's servants still living in the area?"

"None that I can recall. Peter, do you remember anyone?"

"Not any servants, no. But there was that cook. Remember, she came from England with Lady Worthington. Not Mrs. Haughton, but the one who was before her. You know, the old one who had the accident?"

"Mrs. Symes. Yes, old Mrs. Symes. Heavens, she must be in her eighties by now. But I believe she's still alive. Still at the nursing home in Métain, a few miles from here. I was instructed by Her Ladyship to bring a birthday cake, a great big chocolate ganache cake, on her birthday every August. I still do that to this day. I should warn you, Inspector, that she's not quite right in the head.

Fell and had a skull fracture. So, she's a bit—well, she's not exactly all there, you might say."

"I understand then. Tell me, Peter, what was it like being here at the hospital during the war?"

Peter looked away. I noticed he began nervously rubbing his hands along the side of his pocket.

"It was difficult, like everywhere else in France during the occupation."

"Difficult? How so? How was it difficult being at the hospital?"

Peter did not reply. It was Ada who offered, "Well, for one thing, there were difficult discussions with the medical director, Dr. Villmont, about converting the children's hospital into a military hospital for wounded German soldiers. That caused a great deal of anxiety among the staff. Fortunately, that never happened."

"I see. With a conversion to a German military hospital, what were the plans for the children? Were there plans to relocate the patients being treated here? My understanding is that many of the children had chronic neurological conditions that required long-term care."

Ada looked at Peter. "I don't know. Maybe they discussed that. I'm not certain."

Peter jerked his head toward me and said in a firm voice, "They would have all been exterminated. Sent to the camps. Like all the others who the Nazis thought were defective."

I did not reply for a moment, but then I began with, "And what can you tell me about the medical director during this time, Villmont? Would he have allowed this?"

Ada looked at Peter. Peter replied, "He was a collaborator. He would have agreed with whatever the Nazis wanted."

"And what happened to him?"

"He escaped to Lyon. With that other butcher, Barbie. The Maquis got him, but he committed suicide before they could try him."

There was a long silence. I could tell the conversation had brought back uncomfortable memories.

"Thank you very much for your time, Ada and Peter. You've been most helpful."

While the Kunstels indeed had been helpful, I knew a Bavarian accent when I heard one. I'd also begun to pick up an unusual scent I hadn't appreciated before.

After driving back to the hotel, I made a call to the office to reach Guyton. "I want background checks on Dr. Auguste Villmont and Mr. Peter Kunstel from the children's hospital. And I want Kunstel's immigration records."

After liberation on September 14, 1944, General Charles de Gaulle gave a speech at the town hall praising Lyon for being the "capital of the Résistance." This was in no small part thanks to the recognition of Jean Moulin's overall leadership of all underground forces. But Moulin had been betrayed by someone in his inner circle and was captured by the head of the SS in Lyon, Klaus Barbie, the "Butcher of Lyon," who personally had tortured Moulin to death.

The Kunstels had every reason to fear for the lives of the children at the hospital in Saint-Alban. In April 1944, Barbie sent forty-four Jewish children who'd been hiding in an orphanage in Izieu in Southern France to their deaths in Auschwitz.

Barbie personally tortured many of his victims and was directly responsible for the deaths of nearly fourteen thousand individuals. After the war, he was sought by the French authorities as a war criminal, but he escaped capture as he was shielded by the US Counterintelligence Corps. The CIC in 1947 enlisted him as a US agent to search out communists in the French sector. In 1949 the CIC helped smuggle Barbie and his family to South America, where as of this writing, he remains at large, under the protection of right-wing governments.

I have had relatively little experience with nursing homes over the years, as the vast majority of my clients rarely lived long enough

to grace their doors. The ambience at the pensioners' home in
Métain, however, was not at all what I had experienced with Aunt
Béatrice in similar circumstances. When I arrived and showed my
credentials on a chilly but sunny morning in April, it seemed that
all the residents were outside on the terrace with blankets folded
over their laps, carrying on in a quite animated fashion with the
nursing staff. There were multiple bottles of wine on the tables,
raucous laughter, and music. I concluded that this must be some
kind of Valhalla for unrepentant alcoholics.

Mrs. Violet Symes, who was not yet partaking in the festivities,
was stationed in an airy central room watching a television program
while knitting. Violet was a large woman, amply filling out her
wheelchair. Her white hair flowed along the contours of her round,
pleasant face and scarlet cheeks. I convinced the staff to take her
back to her room for a more private conversation.

"Are you really the police?"

"Yes, you could call me that."

"Is this about my Dickie? The lad means well, you know. His
father beat him so."

"No, not at all. I've come here to inquire about Lady
Worthington."

"Her Ladyship! How delightful. Still sends me my birthday
cake. Every year, mind you. Is she well?"

"I'm afraid she's been ill. Did you enjoy your time at the
hospital?"

"Forty years. Oh yes. I did so love the children. Always being
so very cheeky coming into my kitchen for the cookies. I miss
them so!"

"Mrs. Symes, do you remember someone named Jocko?"

"Oh, of course! How Her Ladyship loved that child! His foot
was very crooked, and the doctors in Toulouse made such a mess
of it. She had to call in specialists from Paris and then London to
fix it. Such a sweet boy!"

Just then a nurse came into the room with a small cup.

"Time for your pills, Mrs. Symes."

I waited for the nurse to leave, and then asked my final question:

"Do you happen to recall a priest, a Father Fabien Loriot, who then became archbishop?"

She leaned her head toward me. "Oh yes. That blacky-black man. The priesty-priest. I called him that. His long robes. He wasn't right, that one."

"Wasn't right?"

"Oh yes. He was always there at the hospital on Christmas and holidays. Always there, priesty, messing with the boys. Always bringing sweets. Always the little boys. Never the girls. Priesty-priest always made the little boys sit on his lap. In the library. Made them cry so. 'A private audience with priesty.' No one could go in. Her Ladyship got so cross. They had words. But he wouldn't stop and go away. He always would come back. He's not right, that one. Not right."

There can be no finer exemplar of the intersection of art and criminality than Caravaggio. The baroque genius, who painted for the elite but lived in the shadowy Roman underworld, was particularly fond of depicting scenes of death and blood-spurting beheadings. He scandalized the Carmelites, who had commissioned a painting of the death of the Virgin when they received a portrait of Caravaggio's favorite prostitute lying dead in a modest bedchamber. Fiery-tempered, Caravaggio fled Rome in 1606, when he killed a man while attempting to castrate him in a sword fight after a tennis match. Were the mutilated genitals in the Saint-Alban case an homage to that act?

The archbishop's art collection was of keen interest to me. Over lunch one Tuesday with Emma and Oscar, I asked if they knew anyone at the university who might be acquainted with it. The following day, I had coffee in a café near the old town with Professor Albertini, an expert in Renaissance and baroque art.

"Thank you so much for meeting me on such short notice, Professor."

"Not at all, Inspector. And you must call me Tommasso."

"And please, call me Charles. I was wondering if you'd ever seen the archbishop's art collection?"

"Only once, I'm afraid. I was not visiting in any official capacity as an art historian. It was a social event, a reception put on by the provost of the university to celebrate the archbishop's twenty-fifth year in office. There was an informal tour. I am quite sure the archbishop had no idea of my position. I've called and written many times requesting to come back and bring my students to study the collection, but I've never received a reply."

"What were your impressions of the collection?"

"It was a bit difficult to know what was real and what was not. In my judgment, the main works of significance in his collection are very fine reproductions of paintings by Velázquez and Caravaggio. There were a number of minor Renaissance painters as well. The person conducting the tour freely admitted that many of the works were reproductions. That is no doubt true because many were of paintings that are prominently featured in national galleries. The two Caravaggios, for example: *Boy with a Basket of Fruit* hangs in the Borghese; the *Bacchus* is in the Uffizi."

"Is there anything you can tell me about those specific paintings?"

"Speaking quite frankly, they are two very early examples of Caravaggio's homoerotic art."

"I see. Do you suppose any of the Velázquez paintings are real?"

"Possibly. I'm not sure, but there were a number of smaller works that I didn't recognize. They could be genuine. The brushstrokes have a similarity. Of course, determining the provenance of a painting is a specialty unto itself."

"Is it possible that any of the works in the archbishop's collection were looted from Jewish collectors?"

"I am afraid that can be said of every major art collection in postwar Europe. To my knowledge, though, the archbishop's collection has never been subject to any sort of investigation in that regard."

"I'd like to know a little bit about the subject of crucifixion in Western art. I'm specifically referring to the depiction of an individual being crucified upside down. What can you tell me about that?"

"That is a well-known subject for medieval and Renaissance painters, including Caravaggio. It specifically refers to the upside-down crucifixion of Saint Peter, who did not want his crucifixion to emulate that of Jesus."

"Peter, you said?"

"Yes."

I was concerned that a confidential dossier on the personal life of the archbishop would be especially sensitive in Toulouse, so I had my office in Paris deliver it by special courier. I had been able to obtain both private government records and church records through my contacts. Appreciative though I was, I am always startled to know how much information exists within the files on otherwise upstanding citizens.

The dossier contained a number of salient points. Fabien Loriot was indeed of humble origins, having been given up for adoption when he was little more than a year old. He was raised in a family of six on a farm near Carcassonne. As a boy, he showed great aptitude in school and was able to attend a private Jesuit lycée in Toulouse. He went on to attend university in Bordeaux. He was ordained as a priest at twenty-five and later earned a graduate degree in philology from the Sorbonne. While there is clear evidence of academic distinction, there is no clear record of any financial scholarships. After being a priest in several parishes near Toulouse, he rapidly rose through the clerical ranks, spending five years in administrative posts in the Vatican before becoming a bishop at the ripe age of forty-three.

There were several counseling memos to the file dating back to Loriot's days as a parish priest that referenced "inappropriate behavior," but nothing more. Later, during his career as bishop, there were concerns about lavish entertaining and expensive gifts.

This was a remarkable rise to power for a farmer's son.

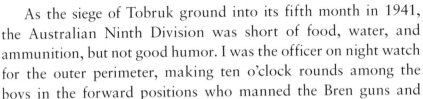

As the siege of Tobruk ground into its fifth month in 1941, the Australian Ninth Division was short of food, water, and ammunition, but not good humor. I was the officer on night watch for the outer perimeter, making ten o'clock rounds among the boys in the forward positions who manned the Bren guns and the antitank artillery. I was especially keen to see how Lieutenant McInness was holding up. A German barrage that afternoon had killed several men in his squad. But it was he who started the conversation.

"Evening, Captain. Was the opera not to your liking, sir?"

"Well, as you no doubt know, Lieutenant, if you've seen one Verdi, you've seen them all. Just making sure your boys are serving the beer at the proper temperature before I take my moonlight swim."

"Right, sir."

"Look, Mac, I was sorry to hear about the lads in your company."

"Right."

"May I help with the letter writing?"

"Thank you, sir, but I'm getting quite good at it these days. Thing is, sir, not one of them was much past twenty. Just lads really. Couldn't grow a beard to save their souls."

One of the few things I had learned in combat was that sometimes the best thing to do is merely to be present and to say nothing. Suddenly, an orange flare shot up over the blackened desert, casting jagged shadows over a reef of destroyed Cromwell tanks, which crested the tops of the dunes like ancient shipwrecks.

"This business with Jerry, sir. When's it going to be over?"

"I think it's still early innings, Mac."

"Thing is, sir, what's an educated man like you doing here? I mean, all of us blokes just do what they tell us to: point the guns and shoot. But you, sir."

I again said nothing.

"Got a wife and kids at home, sir?"

"A sweetheart, you might say."

"That's even better. As long as they don't meet."

From August 1941 until the day my army unit was demobilized in '46, I carried in my wallet a small photograph of Sandy, tucked inside a letter that for the first time she had signed, "Love." I endured a lot of hardship in the desert and in even more in German prison camps, but I knew that late in the evening, if I could glance at that photo and that signature for even a few minutes before they turned off the single light in the barracks, I could endure anything they could throw at me.

I was beginning to feel the same way about Françoise.

It was a Sunday morning in the kitchen, and I was, as usual, washing turnips and peeling potatoes, while Françoise was writing down lists of the combinations of courses she would prepare for dinners in the coming week. She was wearing a pair of beige khakis and one of my white work shirts tied at the waist and open in the front to accommodate her pale peach-colored scarf. Her hair, streaked with black and white, was tucked behind one ear; her elbow was leaning on the kitchen table; and her hand was twirling a pencil.

I kept staring at her for what must have been several minutes, in the most wonderful, rapturous trance, until she looked back and said, "What? What is it?"

In 1804 Marie-Antoine Carême assumed the position of chef for Talleyrand at the Château de Valençay, only after having been given an examination to create daily menus for an entire year without any repetition and using only fresh seasonal ingredients. Needless to say, he passed the test.

One can never overestimate the transcendent importance of French cuisine in nourishing the body. Similarly, one cannot ever overestimate the stirring ideals of the French Revolution in nourishing the body politic.

However, there is an even greater contribution of France and, more specifically, of the Languedoc to the soul of European civilization. That is the concept of personalized romantic love, embodied by the lyric poetry of the twelfth-century troubadours around Toulouse. Their idealized spiritual love for the lady of the castle could never—or perhaps almost never—be consummated. That was not the point. The exquisitely personalized *fin amour* of Languedoc troubadours transcended both the impersonal Eros of biological sexuality and the impersonal love of one's neighbor, or agape, espoused in Christian ethics.

The newfound Western ideal of romantic love for the troubadours was a "seizure of the eyes," an all-encompassing spiritual integration of the senses creating an intensely pure love for one and only one human being.

We were on one of our Sunday strolls. Françoise asked, "Charles, tell me about your family. I mean, you've met my father, my uncle, and my sister, but I hardly feel as if I know who your people are. Your parents, for example—you never talk about them."

Perhaps that is because, at the end of the day, I feel as if I hardly knew them.

"Well, my parents had the good sense of dying in middle age."

"Charles, that's unfair. What were they like? Tell me."

"The conventional kind, I'd say. My father spent most of his waking life consumed with his law practice. My mother spent most of her waking life consumed with either taking vacations or dreaming about her next vacation. Two ships passing in the night. I was mostly raised by my aunts and uncles."

"You mentioned your uncle Carlos once. What was he like?"

Which of the many personas should I reveal?

"A complex sort, but I would say that of all my family, he was the most loving. When I was a young boy, he was the only one who would actually hug me and tell me that he loved me. I remember once when I was around eight years old, Uncle Carlos had somehow misplaced the box that contained all his dry flies for fishing. This was a tragedy of the highest order to my uncle. I spent three hours on Sunday morning scouring our house to find that box. Seems that the maid had misplaced it by putting it in my mother's room. When I returned it to him, you would have thought I'd recovered the crown jewels. He hugged me and kissed me in such a truly genuine way that I felt truly loved—perhaps for the first time."

Up until now.

The x-ray report of the feet of the corpse provided by the pathologist offered a diagnosis of right foot deformity, possibly related to clubfoot. I knew I needed an expert opinion, so I walked into Guyton's office.

"Sergeant Guyton, I want you to have these x-rays sent to Paris by courier tonight to the attention of Professor Henri Matlan at the Roentgen Institute, Hôtel Dieu Hospital."

"Very good, sir. And the immigration file on Mr. Kunstel will be on your desk shortly."

"Anything of interest, Sergeant?"

"Only that I thought you said he claimed to be Dutch, sir."

"He claimed that, yes."

"Well, he actually emigrated from Munich in 1932. His real name is Peter Finebaum."

"Anything surface on Villmont?"

"More than a casual relationship with Pétain. Captured by the Maquis in Lyon. Hung himself before his tribunal."

There is always the misfortune of conflicting information, Charlie. As sharp as it is, remember this: nobody ever sliced his throat open on Occam's razor.
—A.L.

The next morning a call came from the prison in Marseille.

"What did you find, Candy?"

"There are a number of irregularities with the hospital's finances, Inspector. Very suspicious irregularities. After Lady Worthington died in '39, the board of directors took over and ran the place during the war. For some unknown reason, the board right away began to sell off virtually all the land it owned along the Tarn River. By 1946, all the property that remained was the three hundred hectares of the immediate hospital grounds and its hilltop gardens. The sale raised a rather large sum of money. The sum was quite remarkable for a wartime sale. But there is no clear indication what triggered the board to sell. The hospital's endowment was quite sufficient to cover operating expenses. And, in fact, the operating budget of the hospital went down considerably during the war as the full-time staff was cut from fifty to thirty-three. So, the reason for the sale to generate this type of revenue is quite peculiar."

"Do we know who purchased the land?"

"Yes, in fact, we do. There are bills of sale that show that a number of villagers bought the land, as did outsiders from Paris, Rouen, and Bordeaux. But the curious thing is that the villagers paid substantially less per hectare for riverfront property than the outsiders paid for land far removed from the river."

"Quite a hometown discount."

"Yes. And one final point: The hospital raised over 2.5 million francs in the land sale. Nearly 1.4 million was cleverly disguised as quarterly accountant fees and invoices going to a firm called DDS Incorporated. I've made enough inquiries to know the firm does not exist. The real accountants for the hospital have always been a firm in Toulouse, Lavin and Messonnier. To pursue the money trail, I'd be looking for someone or some entity with the initials DDS."

"So, do you know the chair of the wartime board of directors overseeing the sale of this property?"

"Yes. His name is Dumont. Marcel Dumont."

"Excellent work. As a down payment, Candy, you'll soon be receiving a bottle of calvados. Just be careful to be on your best behavior at those Algerian dinner parties."

A call came in the next afternoon from Professor Matlan in Paris.

"Good afternoon, Charles."

"Professor, I greatly appreciate your prompt response."

"Well, it's no trouble really to look at some foot x-rays, especially in light of all you and Freddy have done for the hospital over the years. The annual charity costume ball is just somehow not the same without Freddy. In any case, the radiographs reveal a complicated case of talipes equinovarus, or clubfoot in lay parlance."

"Complicated in what way?"

"There was a series of childhood surgeries on the foot to attempt to correct the deformity—osteotomies or resections of bone. There is also evidence of chronic infection and osteomyelitis resulting from those surgeries. Of course, that entire mode of therapy is outdated today. But this individual must have suffered greatly as a child."

"As would have the parents of that child."

"Undoubtedly. Remember, this all happened prior to the era of antibiotics, so the recovery from this sort of complication would be quite protracted. However, given all the surgeries and the care required for the ensuing infections, well, the parents must have been people of means and extraordinarily devoted to their child."

I reviewed the paperwork relating to the land sales from the hospital, made a list of all the purchasers, and placed the list on Sergeant Guyton's desk. I then went for a walk in the old city. The slanting darkness of the late afternoon cast long shadows across the narrow streets. It seemed to concentrate my mind to a precise, focused space. I thought about the initialism DDS, but nothing came to mind. After a glass of cabernet at the Café Martinique, I placed a call to Sergeant Guyton.

"Sergeant, I've sent you a list of names and addresses of individuals who purchased land from the hospital. I want a description of these individuals with specific reference to their relationship, if any, to the archbishop. I'd like you to give this top priority."

"The report will be on your desk in the morning sir."

<hr />

Charlie, never talk first to the man in charge. Always first question his valet or, better yet, his bartender.
—A.L.

I realized I had clearly violated one of Freddy's maxims in speaking first to the mayor. I realized I needed to go back to Saint-Alban and speak to the bartender at the village café.

"Back so soon, Inspector?"

"Yes. Well, you do have quite an impressive wine list. And you are, monsieur?"

"Jules. Jules Floret."

"Pleased to meet you, Jules. I'll have the local red wine, thank you. I assume you've spent much of your life here?"

"My great-grandfather opened this café, if that's what you're asking."

"Tradition. I like that. Jules, is it just my impression, or are people around this village much more prosperous than most?"

"Some are, some aren't."

"And the villagers who bought the land along the river, are they doing well?"

He fidgeted as he strangled a wineglass with a towel. "Some are, some aren't."

"Quite a number of new homes are being built there. You can see them all along the river road. A lot bigger than the old stone farmhouses. Are those villagers doing well?"

"Oh, those people aren't from Saint-Alban. They're from Paris or Rouen or wherever. Summer homes for them."

"I see. But isn't it true that there were several villagers who originally bought the land?"

"Some of the plots, yes, but they sold them off within a few years."

"So, the villagers who sold the land, did they make a tidy profit from the sale?"

"You could say that. Some did, apparently."

"I'm not sure I understand why the hospital was so generous selling the land along the river. Can you explain that?"

"Perhaps it wasn't what that villagers were buying. Perhaps it's what the archbishop was buying."

"And what was that?"

"You'll have to ask him."

"Of course. Well, you've been very helpful."

I got out my pen and wrote down the name of every conceivable individual related to the case with the initials DDS. It was a short list.

I went to the office first thing in the morning and reviewed the report on my desk from Sergeant Guyton. There were a few details, however, I wished to discuss in person.

"Sergeant, concerning the people on the list, do they have anything in common?"

"Well, sir, the one thing in common among the nine individuals on that list is that they are all current or former members of Saint-Alban's town council."

"I see. Excellent work, Sergeant. Two final things. Take this down. I want you to contact the American War Department of Fine Arts and Archives in Paris and do a background check on an Italian national named Domenico de Silva. I want you to track down any connections to stolen Jewish art. The last thing I want you to do is to obtain a search warrant to search the workshop of Peter Kunstel at the children's hospital. I want it searched tonight. I want you to obtain forensic samples from all the drill bits in the machine shop."

"Yes, sir. What kind of samples are we looking for exactly, sir?"

"Bone fragments."

"Right, sir. If I could have a moment, there's been a development at the children's hospital. A Dr. Remy just called me and said that the archbishop had been there to visit the children this morning. Some sort of an altercation occurred, and he got overly excited and collapsed. He has been transported to Toulouse for a presumed stroke. To the neurology clinic here."

"I see. How serious it is?"

"Haven't heard yet, sir."

I got up from the table and, for some reason, glanced out the window at the street. The morning light was a pale amber, and between the narrow, ancient streets there were long, ribbonlike shadows draping the cobblestones. I could see an old pensioner with a heavy brown overcoat walking down the pavement, unsteady even with his cane. He was a large man, and there was something curiously familiar about the tilt of his wide-brimmed felt hat. He stopped and looked up in my direction for a moment, lifting his cane toward me.

Was it him, an older version of Freddy? I leaned closer to the windowsill to get a better look, but the man was gone. I knew what I had to do.

"Sergeant, listen carefully. I want you to have a squad of plainclothes policemen in position tonight outside the neurology clinic at eight o'clock. Divide your men so that you will have groups watching both the front and rear entrances. They are to be ready to apprehend anyone fleeing the hospital. Is that clear?"

"It's clear, sir."

I had a nondescript lunch at a local bistro and then called Françoise from there to let her know that new information had just come from Paris and I would miss dinner at the hotel. I walked back to my office and retrieved my revolver from the locked drawer.

Things always go wrong in our line of business, Charlie. That's the nature of the beast. Remember, when everything is chaos and out of control, the one thing you must control is yourself.
—A.L.

Later that afternoon I introduced myself to the clinic director, Dr. Binet, and informed him of my concern for the safety of the archbishop. I was informed that the archbishop was partially paralyzed on his right side and that his speech was slightly slurred. The prognosis was uncertain. I then asked to be given an orderly's uniform and to be introduced to the nurse in charge of the neurology ward as the night cleaning person. There was to be nothing to suggest that there was anything out of the ordinary.

The archbishop was in a private room off the main hallway of the third-floor ward. Visiting hours were over at eight, and shortly thereafter the doctor on call and his nurse methodically made evening rounds. In my ill-fitting uniform, I began my long vigil by slowly sweeping the hallway.

One loses track of time in places like this with all the disorienting antiseptic odors, but glancing at the main clock at the nurses' station, I realized that quite a few hours had passed without incident. Just after the end of visiting hours I was jolted out of my stupor by a clacking sound of footsteps in the stairwell. I heard more footsteps. I then saw someone, a man, racing to enter the archbishop's room. He was holding something in his hand. I rushed in and drew my revolver.

"I arrest you, Peter Kunstel, for attempted murder!"

Peter hurled the hatchet toward the archbishop's head. It clanged against the metal railing. He bolted past me, knocking me over, and raced down the stairwell, into the open arms of Sergeant Guyton.

―――◇―――

A murder case, Charlie, is a bit like chatting up a beautiful woman in a bar. You're not quite sure how it's going to go at first, but in the end, you wish it had lasted just a bit longer.
—A.L.

We announced our engagement in June on Oscar's sunlit terrace under a wisteria canopy. Despite her objections, I had refused to let Françoise do any of the cooking and had had the whole event catered with the finest service from the hotel. When the meal was finished, Oscar and I went for a long walk along a path by the woods.

"Why did he do it, Charlie?"

"Peter Kunstel was a German Jew who escaped the Nazis in '32, only to come to the hospital in Saint-Alban to discover that anti-Semitism was alive and well in the Languedoc. He knew that the archbishop not only was a pedophile preying on children in the hospital, but also that he was a major collaborator with the SS. Along with the local parish priest, the archbishop had revealed the hiding places of many prominent Jewish families he had pretended to protect and, in the process, confiscated their art. But the real paintings he craved were by Velázquez. Herman Goering had stolen those himself, so the archbishop raised a small fortune selling off the hospital's landholdings along the river to buy them from Goering through Pétain. He was clever enough to disguise the purchase by going through an intermediary."

"The Italian, De Silva?"

"Yes, exactly."

"Why would Goering want to sell his Velázquez paintings?"

"Apparently paintings of dwarves do not fit the idealized vision of the Aryan master race."

"But the archbishop was investigated after the war. He was cleared, wasn't he?"

"The tribunal whitewashed everything. They were paid off. The witnesses were mostly other local officials and members of Saint-Alban's town council who all had been bribed by having property sold to them along the river at bargain prices."

"But still, Charlie, to fake a crucifixion is an extreme act."

"It was an extreme act because Peter Kunstel was afraid the archbishop would never be held to account and never be brought to justice unless he committed a spectacular crime that would attract major attention. Because of their physical resemblance, Peter sensed there was a connection between the archbishop and Jocko. So, when Jocko died, Peter took his dead body from his cottage and nailed it to the cross. He positioned it at the door of the archbishop's residence precisely because he wanted him to be reinvestigated, not by collaborators from Toulouse, but by the authorities from Paris. By people like me. And in the end, Peter got what he wanted: a thorough outside inquiry. I completed the investigation Peter had wanted all along. Even though the archbishop died of a stroke, all his wrongdoings have since come to light."

"What exactly was the connection between Jocko and the archbishop?"

"Twins, born out of wedlock in Switzerland to the governess, the future Lady Worthington. Lord Worthington needed a male heir to prevent his estate from getting into the hands of his nephew. He had impregnated the governess and, thinking she would be quite fertile, divorced his wife to marry her. The irony was that after the delivery of twins in Switzerland, Lady Worthington developed peritonitis and never again bore him a child."

"I don't understand why she founded a children's hospital."

"Her son Jocko was born with a clubfoot requiring multiple surgeries. She founded the hospital as an elaborate means of ensuring she would always be close to him."

"And her relationship with her son the archbishop?"

"She knew he was a pedophile, but still she bankrolled Loriot's rise."

"And who was this De Silva character?"

"An Italian Fascist art collector who did business with the Nazis."

"In stolen Jewish art?"

"That's correct."

"What about the significance of the Cathar cross?"

"Symbolic of Peter's hatred for Catholics and the archbishop."

"I see."

"And as it turns out, the Cathar priests were repulsed by any and all forms of sexuality, and that explains perhaps—"

"The mutilated genitalia."

"Yes."

"And the upside-down crucifixion? A reference to Saint Peter? In other words, was that Peter's Kunstel's way perhaps of drawing attention to himself and to the fact that he alone had crafted such a truly spectacular crime?"

"Full marks, Oscar. I believe you are now beginning to understand the inner workings of the criminal mind."

The past is not dead. In fact, it's not even past.
—William Faulkner

After I filed the last of my reports documenting the Saint-Alban case, I did what Freddy and I would always do: I went to a quiet café and shared my reflections with a carafe of wine. Ultimately, what had I learned from this case? I kept going over Faulkner's quotation in my mind. While it is admirable and reassuring that classical French cuisine in Lyon has endured with subtle variations throughout the centuries, it is not as edifying to know that many of Europe's darkest undercurrents—from clerical abuse to anti-Semitism, collaboration with evil, and the power of the elites—have likewise endured. Is it too much to hope that some measure of goodness and empathy will somehow manage to drift along in the choppy tide of our shared human history? With that sentiment, I realized that this was the essential role Freddy had played for so many of us.

My mind wandered back to Freddy's funeral, on a blustery, snowy day in January. The church in Montmartre was overflowing, and the unruly crowd poured out onto the surrounding streets. The Parisian police force sat in the four front rows, but we were simply overwhelmed by the huge throng behind us of mobsters, petty criminals, bartenders, and women of the night.

Father Barnard lifted up his arms as he began the service. "Seeing all of you in church here today confirms my faith in miracles."

Albert Dumont was forced to resign his position because of the scandal involving his father. My application for the position was accepted, and I became the chief of police in Toulouse.

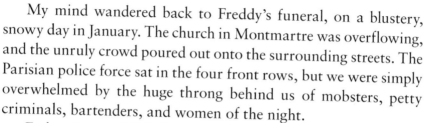

I sometimes take my son Albert with me on a Sunday morning in early summer to fish the mayfly hatch on the Tarn. I try as best as I'm able to teach him how to cast the fly line toward the widening rings of rising trout as Uncle Carlos once taught me. In those quiet moments, I continue to wonder about the paradox, the gruesome case of the crucifixion in Saint-Alban being that which led me to this tranquil place.

In the end we all must strut our brief hour upon the stage. The fortunate among us, such as Freddy, have the courage and determination to dig deep beneath the crust of this world's sorrows in order to reach a life-sustaining aquifer of compassion and understanding, which allows us to connect with our fellow wanderers. The most fortunate of us all, however, meet our Françoise.

Printed in the United States
By Bookmasters